Ludovico's Vengeance

Endgame

The Unexpected Series

The Unexpected Match

The Unexpected First

The Unexpected Reunion

The Unexpected Third

The Unexpected Dance (Coming late 2025)

Mafia Books

Ludovico's Vengeance

Dark Romance

Killer In Our Pocket

Smalltown

Pumpkin Spice and Mr. Right

Ludovico's Vengeance

L. Clara

Contents

Trigger Warnings 

Please note that this book may include but is not limited to the
following trigger and content warnings:

Cheating with partners family member (not main love interest)

Mentions of past trauma as a child

Physical confinement

Severe psychological manipulation

Lack of autonomy

Social Isolation

Feral Child Syndrome

Social withdrawal in childhood

Child Abuse

Child Neglect

Child abandonment

Deprivation of rights and freedom of an individual and/or child

Captive child syndrome

Sexually Explicit Scenes

Bullying (not between main characters)

Death

Murder

Use of multiple weapons

Some torture

Carving skin

***

Bonus Prologue TW

Stalking

Breeding Kink

Your mental health matters more than a book, so please do not read if
any of the above mentioned triggers may negatively affect you.

Another One Bites The Dust – Queen

Cut – Plumb

Scars – Boy Epic

I Found – Amber Run

Control – Zoe Wees

Heal – Tom Odell

Praying – Kesha

I Need You – LeAnn Rimes

Fire – Mike Apt, Steven Rodriguez

Leave a Light On – Tom Walker

I'm Not Alone – Plumb

Saved My Life – Sia

love me – Ex Habit

trouble – Camylio

Start a War – Klergy, Valerie Broussard

Ashes – Celine Dion

If You Love Her – Forest Blakk

Can You Hold Me – NF, Britt Nicole

With the Devil I'm Going Down – Steelfeather

Dark Things – ADONA

Up Down – Boy Epic

The Other Side – Ruelle

Down – Simon, Trella

Father Figure – George Michael

Who Will Save You – Katie Garfield, Obeds

This Love – Novi

I Can Love You Like That – All-4-One

Just You And I – Juniper

Fottuto Stronzo - Fucking Asshole

Bella – Beautiful

Amore Mio - My Love

Via Mia – My Life

Sei mio – You're mine

Sì, tuo – Yes, yours

Amore mio, stasera mi costringerai a uccidere qualcuno – My love,

You're going to make me kill someone tonight.

For the people who have been forced into the shadows...
Let's light this motherfucker up.

"Nothing can prepare you for the moment you find your fiancé in bed with your grandfather. To see the man who you have spent your entire life emulating, balls deep in the woman you have sworn your life, heart, and allegiance to." I take a breath, getting lost in the awful and chaotic memory. "My entire future came to a crashing halt at that moment. And, if you had asked my mother at the time; that was a problem."

The older man before me is hunched over and groaning as he tries to catch his breath. His olive toned skin appears to be aged from sun damage, more so than one would expect from the type of life he's lived. The metal chair he's tied to is strong enough to keep his large frame in place while I explain myself. At least, until I'm ready to be finished with him.

"Why is it a problem, you ask?" Not that he did ask, but I can't help the smirk that pulls at the corner of my mouth.

His dark hair has begun to turn silver at his temples giving him a Josh Duhamel look, granted, not attractive like Mr. Duhamel. What? I'm comfortable enough with my sexuality to be able to admit when another man is good looking.

"That would be, because my entire life had already been planned out before I was even conceived." I chuckle as his eyes dart up to my face, shooting daggers. Hmm, if looks could kill. Lucky for me, they can't.

"You see, I was born Giovanni Ludovico into a family that would give Don Corleone a reason to pause. Although, I'll admit, the horse head was a bit much for me to stomach." A powerful shudder rolls through my body. "You just don't fuck with women, children, or animals - that's just basic human fucking decency after all. Not that you'd understand anything about that, right?"

I lean against the cold concrete wall behind me. My arms crossed tightly at my chest as I wait for some type of acknowledgement. Of course, the piece of shit would never give me the satisfaction of admitting what a terrible excuse of a human being he is.

"After the ultimate betrayal from my grandfather and the woman who I thought was the love of my life, I just couldn't remain in the family business. That's why I left and changed my name to the English translation." A deep rumble of laughter reverberates through my chest, "It wasn't a clever change, I know. I'm also aware that my family has likely been tracking me from the moment they realized I had left, but I needed to get away. I've been known as Johnny Lewis for fifteen years now."

An exasperated sigh leaves my lips before I continue.

"It's been my time as Johnny that has brought me back home." The man remains motionless as his eyes bore into me. I may keep my mask of indifference in place, but internally I'm reveling in his visible rage.

"I had befriended a few people when I started my own law firm eight years ago in a fairly small city, Central Falls." I lift my shoulders in a shrug, "One of those people just so happened to be married to a goddess of a woman. I may have developed a bit of a crush, so I avoided her." A genuine smile tugs at my lips as I remember Hadley, a beautiful woman who has a fuck ton of strength to overcome what she has been through. I had befriended her husband not long after I moved to Central Falls, that was until he became my client and I transitioned the relationship to strictly professional. Granted, that was mostly because I had such a strong attraction to his wife, and I was thankful as hell that I had an excuse to remove myself from the friendship. "After what I experienced with Lucia, I couldn't bring myself to be around any woman I found attractive. Until he confided in me that he had been cheating on her and beaten her to within an inch of her life. That wasn't how I expected to be brought back into the fold. But, alas, here we are."

I lift my hand in front of my face to inspect my nails, as if I care about how dirty my hands are right now. I'll wash them later; it's just about the theatrics right now.

"My best friend, Milo, is the one who organized his death for me at my mother's request." I roll my eyes, "A request she only made after I agreed to return to the family business. The deal being, I get to end Frederico Ludovico myself upon my return."

Pride fills me when the memory of the man I once longed to be lay bloody and dead in a heap at my feet flashes in my mind.

"I may have been a bit overzealous in the way I handled that, if I'm honest. I've never been a huge fan of the bloody side of the business. Don't get me wrong," I wink at him, "I can make a motherfucker bleed alongside the best of my men; I just choose not to most of the time. I'm sure you already understand that though."

We spend a few moments in silence, disappointment rushes through me as I still get no reaction. What a shame.

"Frederico was my first in such a long time, as you can tell, I only dust off these skills for special occasions. Or well, special pieces of shit; such as yourself."

I drag my blood stained fingers through my hair as I think about everything that's happened since I killed the head of the Ludovico family.

"Well, damn I'm getting ahead of myself. Allow me to begin from when I arrived at the Ludovico mansion."

Six months ago

Anger and tension radiate through my body as I take in the surroundings along the driveway to my childhood home. Memories I had once been so fond of, are now tainted by what Frederico had done to me fifteen years ago. Not much has changed on the exterior of the Ludovico estate. Let's be honest, it's a fucking mansion, whoever says otherwise is trying to be humble when they are likely unable to even define the word.

Bright green grass makes up the expansive acreage apart from the circular drive. Large Princesse Charlene de Monaco rose bushes line the right side — my Nonna had insisted upon it for privacy. She had told me once the pastel peach color of flowers that bloom from these bushes were her favorite and wanted to be surrounded by them. It wasn't until years later that she admitted that she heard the specific type of rose signified elegance. Nonna Ludovico was the embodiment of elegance within the world she belonged to. No one, not even Frederico, would question her. He didn't become the filth I know today until well after she passed away. At least, not outwardly. If Nonna could see what he's done, she would roll over in her grave.

My car slows as I press my right foot down on the brake when I get closer to the front steps. When I finally shift into park, I sit for several minutes on my own. As I take in the last moments of what little solace I've had since I made the decision to come home, I realize, this is it. This is the beginning of his end. Strangely enough, that fact gives me more peace than I would expect.

A gust of wind picks up the moment I pull the door handle to step out of my car. The heavy metal barrier nearly drags me out of the car as it's forced open so wide by the gusts that it tests the hinges. Shit, I have not missed this place. My fingers grip around the handle of my duffle bag on the passenger seat and I pull it out of the car behind me as I step outside. Straightening my spine, I begin walking toward the front door, my steps are full of more confidence than I feel.

As I approach the oversized dark-oak wood and glass panel arched door, both sides fly open. My mother, the ever-flawless Giovanna Ludovico – yes, she had a Gilmore Girls moment when I was born and named me after herself – stands before me with her arms wide. Her long dark hair cascades in soft waves over her shoulders. Soft wrinkles at the corner of her light brown eyes, which match mine, is the only thing that shows her age.

"*Vita mio!*" She rushes, wrapping herself around me.

My heart crumbles into a thousand pieces. I hadn't realized just how much I've missed this woman until I feel her warmth against me. And her heart beating alongside mine.

"*Madre,*" I whisper into her hair as I squeeze her tight against my chest.

A throat clears from the doorway, I glance up to find Milo, my best friend since high school, standing there with a shit eating grin spread across his face. My own excitement over seeing him is matched in my expression. Her arm loosens its hold as my mother releases me and steps aside so Milo and I can pull one another into an embrace.

"Man, is it good to see you, Gio!" His voice is more gruff than usual as he speaks into my shoulder.

When we finally release one another, I shake my head, the smile still firmly in place. I can't believe the man that is standing in front of me was once the scrawny punk I had to get out of trouble more times than I can count. He's filled out since I last saw him, now with a broad chest and shoulders straining against his black button up like a beast. I wonder if his trainer can hold a candle to Clay.

"You too, Milo – but, it's Johnny now." I correct him.

My mother's eyes glisten with tears at my statement. Inwardly I'm groaning, however, I keep my annoyance masked. I know she wasn't happy when I changed my name, but it was a necessary evil to be able to separate myself from the lot of them. And, well – I'm not Giovanni and I haven't been for a long time.

No one bothers to acknowledge my correction; Milo simply moves aside to allow me access to the house. It's exactly as I remember. I step inside, into the large foyer furnished with overstated antiques from my grandparents and great grandparents, years of collecting take up space all around the entryway. As I continue through the space, I see a chest I once hid in for a game of hide and seek when my father was still alive. But, we don't talk about him.

"Where is he?" I ask as I continue my way through my childhood home into the large living room. My eyes linger on the sizeable floor length windows, which take up the entire east side wall of the room. The view of the front drive and oversized yard is impressive from this angle. You can see so much of our expansive land. The rose bushes are just the start of the vast estate.

When no one answers, I turn back to look at my mother and my friend. My eyes dart back and forth between the two before she breaks the silence.

"He and Lucia are in Sicily for the week."

My blood becomes molten in my veins as I allow her words to sink in. He is still with the woman I was supposed to marry.

"Why the fuck didn't you tell me?" I snarl at them both.

Milo steps between Giovanna and I before he finds his nerve to speak.

"Because she will be a non-issue after this trip." His dark eyes penetrate through my anger, and I step back as if I've been slapped.

"What in the actual fuck, Milo. We don't kill women." The words come out in a feral growl.

He shakes his head as if I've misunderstood. How the fuck could I misunderstand what he's just admitted to me.

"No, Gi-Johnny. We're not killing her." He shakes his head, an amused expression etched across his face. "Frederico is leaving her there, he's offered her to one of the soldiers in the old country. She just won't know until she wakes up and he's gone."

The words pierce through my rage, and I begin to laugh. It's an unfamiliar feeling, a deep rumble of laughter that reverberates through my bones.

"Fuck, that is brilliant. I can't imagine a better revenge for Lucia quite honestly." I admit through the laughter.

After I catch my breath, I slide onto the large red leather couch. My mother takes a seat next to me while Milo is seated opposite me.

"Are we going to discuss the reason you brought me home or am I supposed to guess?" I ask, cutting straight to the point.

Milo snorts and shakes his head. "Never one to pussy foot around a topic. Fuck, it's good to have you home."

My mother shoots a venomous glare at Milo, which makes us both chuckle. However, she's the one who gets into what she wants before my friend and I can get lost in the good ole times we've shared.

"Everyone who matters is in on it. As soon as he gets home, he'll be told there is someone in the cell that he needs to handle." I cock a brow at her in question, she shakes her head, immediately understanding the unspoken concern as she continues. "Don't worry, his arthritis is so bad he can't shoot anymore."

I nod in understanding as I shove my hand into my pocket, feeling the weight of my Roma blade. The knowledge of what we're going to do has me anxious with such anticipation, every scenario running through my mind.

"How many people who don't know will be in the room?" I ask as I see a familiar face approaching the three of us.

Chapter 2
Johnny

"My sweet boy!" Mrs. De Luca, the same housekeeper that has been here since I was a child, calls me the very same endearment from all those years ago. She never did give up on that, even after I grew up. She looks the same as when I last saw her, save for some wrinkles, to be expected with as much time that's passed. I remember when she first came to us. I was only five years old and an absolute handful. She never let that sway her from becoming my safe space. She was more of a nanny back then. As I grew, her duties shifted away from childcare to caring for the house.

I jump to my feet and stride toward her, my arms snake around her round frame. She's more than a foot shorter than my towering six foot five. She still smells like cinnamon, brown sugar, and coffee. A soft chuckle escapes as I squeeze her once more.

"Some things never change; you still smell like cinnamon rolls." I say into her hair before allowing her space. She smiles brightly up at me; her green eyes have the same air of mischief as they did when I was growing up. The pranks we would play on one another used to be the highlight of my days as a kid.

"Oh, that will never change, child. It's a staple in this house. You should remember that, no matter how long it's been." She pinches my side and huffs out her annoyance. "It seems like you and Milo both spend too much time at the gym. I need to put some meat back on our boys' bones." She winks at my mother who rolls her eyes at the comment.

I shake my head and let out another laugh. Mrs. De Luca excuses herself back into the kitchen allowing the three of us to continue our conversation. As I return to my seat on the couch, my imagination runs wild with the possibilities of how this can go down.

"No matter how you decide to do it," my mother begins her explanation again. "We have a car where we will stage the body. Once it's detonated, anyone not in the know will think it was a car bombing."

My brows shoot up.

"Don't you think that will cause a fucking war?" Before I can jump to my feet her hand is on my knee keeping me in place.

Milo snorts, shaking his head as he waits for her to continue. My eyes dart between the two of them. I know I had asked him to protect her while I was gone, but he seems more comfortable around her than I'd like.

"*Idiota.*" My mother scoffs, throwing her hands in the air like she's already fed up with my shit. Fuck, I haven't even been back for an hour. "Don't you think I would put plans in motion to avoid an all-out war? The Espositos will be putting one of their problem soldiers on the chopping block as a scapegoat."

My eyes go wide, shock is an understatement of my reaction to this revelation. She didn't just say that. The Espositos of all people? My heart beats erratically in my chest as I process her words. There's absolutely no way! I know my face is showing my every thought when Milo speaks up for the first time.

"They know Lucia won't be back. That part was their idea, actually. We just suggested it to Frederico." He snorts and drags a hand through his short beard. "The old man doesn't want her to have the family's money, so that part was easy. And on top of that, her family doesn't want to be associated with her after what she did to you. Especially now that you are back." Milo shrugs nonchalantly, as if to say none of what he's telling me is a big deal.

With so much information thrown at me I spend the next few hours digesting it all in my room. Not much has changed since I left. I toss my bag on the chair in the corner before I collapse on the bed. The knowledge of what I'm going to do in just one day's time has my stomach in my throat. It's not like it's the first time I've killed someone. Fuck, I've taken more lives than I care to count which is why I went into law. I wanted to put men like me behind bars; a way to atone for my crimes. Even with my past ...transgressions. Yeah, let's go with transgressions; my wildest dreams couldn't have prepared me for what I'm about to do.

A soft knock on my door pulls me from my thoughts. Mrs. De Luca gingerly presses the solid oak door open. A soft smile on her lips as she crosses the room and places a cup of coffee and white saucer with a cinnamon bun on my nightstand without saying a word. She winks at me knowingly before she steps back out of the room.

I can't help but chuckle, as close as my mother and I are, I've always been closer to Mrs. De Luca. She was married to one of Frederico's enforcers who was killed in a drive-by not long after she started working for us. She never remarried and never had children of her own, but she took me under her wing as if she were a second mom.

Once I've scooted so that my back rests against the headboard, I take a sip of coffee. God, I love Mud House. The owner could roast a mean bean, but damn. No one can make a cup of coffee like Mrs. De Luca. I cautiously set the cup back on the bedside table and lift the cinnamon bun to my lips.

My mouth begins to water just from the scent. My tongue darts out to moisten my lips in preparation for the heaven that is about to touch my tongue. As soon as I take a bite, even more memories return with a vengeance.

Chapter 3
Johnny

Sunlight filters through the curtains slowly pulling me out of un-consciousness. My eyes flutter open through the sleepy haze. A sharp knock sounds on my door seconds before Milo strolls in. I sit up in a rush, the sheet pooling around my waist, goosebumps cover my bare chest as a gust of wind from the air vent washes over me.

"It's time. He'll be here in twenty minutes." My best friend explains his reason for barging in like he owns the fucking place. He's already dressed in the usual dark suit and button up. *Did this motherfucker even sleep?*

I nod and swing my legs over the side of my bed, I groan as a mug of piping hot coffee is shoved into my face. My brows furrow with confusion as I glare up at him. Milo lets out a throaty laugh as he drags it out of reach.

"I figured you'd want a quick jolt before you finally get your revenge." He smirks and places the cup on the bedside table.

I roll my eyes at him and stand, stretching my arms over my head, and walk toward the bathroom with a calm that should make me feel uncomfortable. However, after the memories that surfaced last night, I'm looking forward to this. I don't bother with a shower, just a quick piss to relieve my bladder before pulling on some dark sweats so that we won't have to worry about blood stains after the fact. My gaze darts to the glint of light that hits the silver of my knife handle laying on the bedside table. I smirk and lift it into my hand, testing the weight in my palm before sliding it into my pocket.

"Let's get this done." I grin as I finally pick up the coffee and take a sip of the steaming liquid. An appreciative groan escapes. "Fuck, no one can make a cup like Mrs. D can." My friend grunts and nods in agreement as I take another swig.

Milo and I walk the length of the house to the basement steps. We pass by a handful of soldiers, most of whom seem to be new recruits. No one speaks to me as we pass, but I can feel their eyes following us. When we reach the basement door, Milo pulls the heavy barrier to allow me past the threshold first to head down the stairs. As I descend the steps, I notice a familiar face peeking up at me.

A large figure emerges from the shadows with a wide grin on his lips as he holds out a hand to greet me. I ignore the gesture and pull him into a hug. He chuckles and shoves me away.

"I've missed you too kid, but we can get reacquainted once this is done." Michael Messina, the man who was the closest thing to an uncle I had growing up, says to me. He was my Nonna's favorite of Frederico's men when I was a kid. For a long time, she had hoped that my mother would end up with him since he's only a few years older. His charcoal color hair is still dark and cropped short, it's as if time has stood still, I notice as I take in his features.

My joy at reuniting with someone I have such fond memories of sours when Milo's voice cuts through the room.

"Incoming." He snaps.

I take my position, replacing Michael in the shadows. My eyes flicker to movement in the cell that they'll be leading him into. Someone is hunched over on the floor in the far corner. I grin when I realize it's Michael who has made himself impossibly small, he's nearly unrecognizable from this position.

Moments later, the man of my nightmares is led into the space. He grumbles something in Italian as he approaches the cell. It's not until he's through the open door that I make myself known. Straightening my spine, I make myself taller and quietly approach the scene before me.

"Who the fuck do you think you are to steal from the Ludovico family?" Frederico growls, his voice coming out a bit raspy. He must have gone hard on the cigars for the past decade or so.

Once I'm standing in the doorway, I clear my throat. The same man I looked up to for years, did everything I could to become who he wanted me to be, spins to face me. Looking into his eyes, I remember everything. Every request, every command. Nothing was ever too much. He was a king among men, untouchable, unquestionable. But now, I see him through clear eyes for the piece of shit he is. An insect that must be crushed.

"Everyone, out." I shout with a tone I know my grandfather recognizes. He is the one who taught me how to force those around me to respect my authority as the rightful heir to our family. His face drains of color the moment realization sinks in. "Time's up, old man."

I feel my lips twitch into a sadistic smile as I ball my hand into a fist and throw a right hook. The old man collapses as soon as my knuckles land on the intended mark. Luckily for him, Michael is standing behind him and catches him before he can obtain any real damage from hitting the concrete. Milo drags a metal chair over to the center of the room. The two of them make fast work of restraining him to the chair. Not that I'm worried he could get away or that he could hurt me. It's more for us, so that we don't have to hold him up from falling over until he comes to.

Michael steps out of the cell for a moment leaving Milo and I alone with a still very unconscious Frederico. He returns quickly with something in his hand. As Michael approaches my grandfather, he snaps whatever it is with his fingers. He waves it under Frederico's nose causing him to immediately jolt awake and violently thrash in the chair with what sounds like a painful bit of coughing. I cock a questioning brow in Michael's direction.

"Smelling salts. We don't use them too often; usually we don't care if they wake up." Milo answers me with a shrug of his shoulders.

Understanding dawns and I nod in response. Frederico's eyes find me the moment he has control of his faculties again.

"Giovanni, what are you doing here?" He snarls at me from his place on the metal chair.

Laughter erupts from deep within my chest. He can't be serious. Oh, this is going to be fun.

"It's been a while, Gramps." I reply with a sharpness in my tone as I approach the chair he's seated on. He's too old and from the looks of it, far too fragile to try to get out of his restraints, but based on the hatred in his eyes, he wants to. Oh, does he want to. "I haven't been Giovanni for quite some time, but now that I'm home, maybe he'll have to come out to play and see how much he remembers from your training. After all, the first-time I had been in this very room was the night I found you attacking a man with a bag over his head in this same chair. You made me help you eliminate him when you caught me."

Frederico's eyes go even wider than before. His body begins to shudder as the shock of my memory returning really seeps into his core.

"Do you remember that? The way the metal scraped against the cement floor? His muffled cries from the gag you had in his mouth? I didn't, not until last night." I stifle back a laugh, "after Mrs. De Luca's cinnamon bun, of all things, triggered the memory."

Milo and Michael are still behind me. Neither of them knows. Michael had been assigned to my mother who was away that night for a charity function. Milo and I hadn't met then, I was only a child.

"I guess it makes sense, since it was her husband who was here, helping you. That is, until you forced me to take a knife to my own father's throat." I shoot the words at him like poison. "When you removed the bag and showed me the identity of who I helped you kill, you told me that I was just having a bad dream. Dad had gone out with my mother that night. You even cleaned me up and tucked me in."

My shoulders release tension I didn't realize I've been carrying for so long. Michael lunges for Frederico, but doesn't get far. Milo inserts himself between the two men and nods at me with a knowing look in his eyes.

"See, I had believed you for so long. Fuck, I thought that I wanted to be you for Christ's sake. The moment I saw you with Lucia though. That was simultaneously the best and worst day of my life. I lost so much time with people I love because I couldn't bear to see either of your faces." I pause briefly to take a breath as my explanation marinates in his thick skull. "It wasn't until I was taking notes in a Tort class while I was enrolled in law school that it dawned on me. You were jealous that I showed more promise as a leader than you ever have. Your men respected me back then, even more than they respected you. If it weren't for my mother asking me to let you live because you were still her father, this would have happened fifteen God damn years ago."

I shove my hand into my pocket and wrap my fingers around the handle of my knife. No words are exchanged in the seconds it takes for me to remove the knife from my pants. I press the button to eject the blade from its cover and swiftly slit through my grandfather's throat, just like he had me do to my father all those years ago.

"Jesus fuck." Milo says as the blood flows quickly, pooling at Frederico's feet which just so happen to be right by the drain we use to remove evidence.

I step close enough to tear open the shirt of my now deceased grandfather and carve the calling card the Esposito family uses in this situation. The body may be being placed into a car with an explosive device, but we take precautions. You never know what could happen. With a steady hand, I carve a perfect "E" into the chest followed by an S made of straight lines at a slant. How their men do this on skin when you have to pass over already sliced skin is beyond me. It takes more talent and patience than I'll ever have.

 Chapter 4 — Johnny

The past seventy-two hours have been a revolving door of heads from the different local families visiting with offers of condolences, prayers, and paying their respects. While I understand and respect that part of this life, fuck, I just want to forget about the old man. A loud groan barrels its way from my throat when another knock sounds on the door to what is now my study.

"What?" I ground out as I sift through records from the time I was gone.

A soft creek echoes through the room as Mrs. De Luca steps in with a glass of water and a plate of grilled chicken over a bed of lettuce. I can't help but grin when I see her. She's not spoken to me much since everything came back to me, so it surprises me when she doesn't move to leave right away.

"My sweet boy." She says softly, "Thank you. My Anthony felt so guilty after, he didn't know what Frederico had planned until it was too late. He confided in me when he came home after it was done. Anthony planned to resign, but he never returned the day he intended to ask to be relieved of duty."

Her shoulders sag as she shares her story. I stand from behind my desk and close the distance between the two of us. My arms fold around her in a tight embrace as she quietly sobs into my sternum. Her signature cinnamon and vanilla scent invades my lungs before she pulls away, pats my chest, and walks out without another word shared between us.

A few moments after I've finished my lunch from Mrs. D, a quick succession of knocks in the beat of *Another One Bites The Dust* sounds against the large barrier. I can't help but chuckle.

"Come in, Milo." My shoulders shake with laughter at his antics. He may be in a higher position of power now as my right hand alongside Michael, but he's still the same kid I met all those years ago. Some things will never change.

Milo pushes open the door with a cheesy smile on his face as if he owns the place. Once he steps through the door, he clears his throat.

"Mateo Barone is here to see you." He steps to the drink cart and pours himself a glass of bourbon. "He says it's to express his sympathy for the family, but something feels off." Milo's statement piques my interest.

I drag my hand through my short beard and glance at my friend. I give a quick nod toward the door, Milo turns back to fetch my guest. While I'm waiting for them to return, my attention is drawn to a stack of papers on my desk. Something sticks out like a sore fucking thumb. I hear Milo and Mr. Barone enter before I have a chance to dig in any further. My eyes raise to find an older man with a very large frame, his hair is cropped short at the sides, a little longer on top. However, his temples have gone completely grey.

"Mr. Barone," I ask as I gesture for him to take a seat at the chair in front of my desk, which he does while Milo stands at the doorway with his arms crossed in front of his chest. "How may I help you?"

The older man sits with an expression I can't quite pinpoint. He has more of a street look to him than most of the men who we associate with. Instead of the suit and tie I've become accustomed to seeing over the years, he's wearing a black T-shirt and jeans. Don't get me wrong, casual clothes are great, but not in this environment. I cock a brow at him when he doesn't speak, which must get the point across that I won't break first.

"Giovanni," he begins.

I hold my hand in the air to stop him.

"It's Mr. Ludovico to you, we aren't friends, sir." I reply coldly.

Mr. Barone's lip curls as if he's holding back an insult or two. Good, I'm under his skin.

"Mr. Ludovico," He begins again, "I wanted to pay my respects to you and offer my sincerest condolences to you and your family."

I nod in response. Milo is right, there is something off about this one. He's here for more than what he claims. When I don't verbally acknowledge his statement, he continues.

"A few years ago, your grandfather and I went into business together." The man's gaze darts between Milo and myself as he speaks, "I want to assure you that I will continue to do my part, with your approval to do so, of course." He explains. I cross my arms over my chest and cock a brow at him. "My part with distribution, I mean."

My face heats as a molten rage rushes through my veins as I quickly stand and loom over the man before me. He's at least smart enough to look a little taken aback at my reaction.

"I need you to spell it out for me because the first thing that comes to mind can't be what you're fucking talking about." He staggers backward at my response.

"We - he - I mean, I - we had an - an agreement. It's primarily cocaine and heroin, nothing stronger than those two." Mr. Barone stumbles over his words.

My glare has him cowering into himself as I speak.

"In all the years we've had control, it has been made clear by my great grandfather that we do not dabble in drugs." I snarl as I stand at my full height, my spine straight as an arrow. My chest puffs out to make my appearance more intimidating. "You're telling me that you and Frederico had a deal to get drugs on my streets?"

Milo begins to advance toward me to grab ahold of the man who has been placed at the top of my shit list. I shake my head so quickly, only my friend sees the movement. Milo stays in place allowing it to play out the way it's meant to.

"He approached me about the partnership after he found out." Mr. Barone explains, his voice cracks before he goes silent when he realizes what he gave me.

The hair on my neck stands on end as his words sink in. What the fuck is this man into?

"Found out what exactly?" I snarl; Milo has moved forward with his palms pressing down on Mr. Barone's shoulders, holding him in place. I see the wheels turning behind his eyes as he tries to determine if he can lie to me. He must decide it's not worth it after a few moments of silence, but what he says is not at all what I expect.

"About my daughter." His response is quiet. "No one else knows outside of the woman who raised and tutored her."

I take a step back to take in the whole picture keeping an indifferent mask in place.

"What does your daughter have to do with anything?" I ask as I drag my fingers through my short beard.

Mr. Barone huffs out an annoyed sigh.

"It was supposed to be a boy. I never wanted a girl. I told everyone the baby and her mother died during labor twenty-five years ago." The way he says the words as if it should be self-explanatory shocks me. "We killed her mother since she was worthless, and couldn't produce an heir. My father wouldn't let me get rid of her in case she could become useful down the line."

I glance at Milo whose eyes are now as wide as mine. What. The. Fuck?

The horrors that flash through my mind for a person to be isolated for so long make my stomach flip. Where has this girl been all this time? How old is she? I don't recall ever hearing about a wife and pregnancy before. The blood boils in my veins as I level him with a glare. Mr. Barone flinches as soon as he sees my expression. Good.

"If you want me to consider the remote possibility of you continuing on the venture you started with Frederico, I want your daughter. My men will be escorting you home and retrieving her," I say without hesitation.

Chapter 5

Hot water beats against my skin as I stand under the pulsing jets shooting from the shower head. I like to keep it on the highest setting of pressure that I can. After an hour of my favorite workout, the repetitive pounding from the stream of water beating against my muscles feels so good. Not that I would know what a massage feels like but, I imagine it's a similar sensation. And boy, could I use one, especially after days like today.

My entire body is vibrating with discomfort and soreness. An hour of repeatedly punching a bag that does nothing but mock me will do that to a girl. Yes, I know it's an inanimate object which has been in the corner of my room for as long as I can remember. However, it's annoying, especially when I have no one to spar with like in the videos Cece has shown me. Plus, I hate cardio. I'd rather work with the free weights that I've been granted permission to use every other day. Unfortunately, Cece says I'm not allowed to have them without supervision. Seems dumb to me. But I guess, what do I know?

I grab the bottle of body wash and squirt a dollop onto my loofah before lathering my body up with soap. More often than not, I will spend an exorbitant amount of time taking a long shower; however, something is off today. It feels like if I don't have my eyes on my surroundings, everything is going to be pulled out from under me. Though, I guess since I've never been outside of my room, a change would be nice. Hell, I only have one large window which overlooks the backyard. If I'm honest, I'm mostly forced away from that window.

Besides Cece, my dad is the only other person who I get to see. I've asked about my mom over the years, but I'm met with silence or a handprint across my face. So, I've stopped asking. However, my father is usually so busy with his work, it's rare I get to see him more than once a month. It's been explained to me repeatedly that I'm safest here. The dangers of the outside world should scare me, but the longer I'm forced to stay here, the harder it is. I crave companionship. I love the books that Cece has brought me over the years. But a girl can only handle so many stories that I've never had the chance to experience in life, ya know?

My twenty-fifth birthday is in a few weeks, I'm hoping they'll let me at least step foot into the back yard. Even for just a moment, I've never felt the grass between my toes. It sounds like it could be heaven, to smell the fresh outside air for more than a few moments a day when we open the window.

When I step out of the shower, I grab the towel from the vanity and wrap it around my body. After dragging a brush quickly through my hair, I hear shouts coming from strange voices on the other side of the wall. I pull the towel tight as I step back into the shower and press myself against the cold wet tile. My body trembles as terror begins to take hold of my senses. Whatever is happening out there can't be good. Tears stream down my freshly washed face as a harsh hand bangs against my bathroom door.

"Nina! Get your ass out here." Dad's gruff voice snarls loudly through the thin barrier.

I take a deep breath when I realize I'm safe and let him know that I'll be out in a minute. After I go through a speed round of towel drying my body, followed by my hair, I pull on the matching set of sweatshirt and pants I brought into the bathroom with me. A bright grin spreads across my face when I open the door, it's been so long since I've seen my dad. Instead of who I expect, I see a group of strange tall and muscular copy and pasted men surrounding my father. They're all dressed in identical suits.

"Daddy? I – What's going on?" I take a step back, further into the bathroom which has suddenly become even more of a sanctuary.

"You're no longer my problem." He shrugs and rolls his eyes as he steps aside and all I see is the wall of men I've never met before in front of me. One begins to approach me as I cower into myself.

I scream so loudly my voice cracks when Cece comes running, her plump petite figure barrels through the men, not giving a care in the world at what may come of her disobedience to my father.

"Nina, honey it's ok. They won't hurt you." She whispers gently to me as she tucks a stray strand of her blonde hair back into her messy bun. "I know it doesn't make sense right now, but one day it will. Just go with them, please."

It's the first time in years that Cece has been so openly kind in front of my father. The last time she was like this in front of him, I didn't get to see her for a few days. When I would wake up in the mornings during that time, a cooler with food for the day would be left for me to eat. Since then, she stays silent when he's around. Almost as if I don't exist.

I glance around at the men when one of them steps forward with his hands held up in front of him to show me he's not a threat. He's more beautiful than the others, a square jaw with piercing deep chocolate colored eyes that don't leave mine.

"Hi Nina, I'm Milo." His voice is so smooth and calming that I feel at ease as he speaks. "I promise you, we're not here to hurt you. Your dad has asked us to take you and your things with us to my boss' house. He will explain everything to you when we get there."

Tears are falling uncontrollably now, everything around me becomes a wet and soggy blur. I sense him step forward, and I freeze. I've never been around anyone but Cece and my dad, what am I supposed to do?

"Is it ok if I lead you outside? We have a car waiting to drive you." He explains calmly.

I instantly perk up at the words. Outside? Drive? I feel like those videos I've seen of dogs being teased by their favorite words.

"I get to go outside?" The confusion in my voice has a wicked growl emanating from his chest, which makes me step back again and I find myself pressed against the wall.

Milo steps forward and whispers just loud enough for me to hear.

"Nina, once we get you out of here, you'll be able to go outside whenever you want, but I need you to come with me. Please."

And just like that, my decision to leave the only home I've ever known with people I've never met is made.

Mrs. De Luca has taken it upon herself to prepare the Barone girl's room just down the hall from my own. I don't know much about the girl. After I told Mr. Barone that I wanted her under my roof, he shut down. Not that any of that matters. With the information provided, I know she's turning twenty-five soon and from how the fucker spoke about her, she'll be better off here. Besides, my mother has always wanted a daughter, so she'll be thrilled to have another female around the house that she and Mrs. D can care for.

My men are tasked with fetching the girl while I'm out handling business, which I can't hold off. The desire to end this shit sooner rather than later is what motivates me to get it done as soon as possible —which happens to be today. Mateo was asked to confirm who has been dealing with him and Frederico before I allowed him to leave so that he could assist in his daughter's transition into my custody. Now I'm sitting in the back of a large black SUV while Michael drives me through town.

I take in the rolling hills of the countryside as we drive along the back roads into the city, a drive I remember accompanying my grandfather on time and time again. As we enter the city limits, my gaze is locked on the landmarks from my childhood. Not much is different, yet it feels like everything has changed since I was last here. The same ice cream place is on the corner that my parents took me to as a kid when times were simpler. I blink rapidly as the car begins to slow in front of the old pharmaceutical manufacturing plant.

My, oh my, how things have changed.

When I step out of the car and look up at the side of the familiar building, I see a neon light shaped like a prescription label for the night club that has taken over the space. My eyes shoot to Michael who steps out of the driver seat a moment later.

"Really? They named it 'Rx'?" My lips twist into a smirk as I shake my head. "I'll give them this much, it is clever."

The blinding sun is still high in the sky as I follow Michael through the front doors of the club. As we walk through the entrance, all of the lights are on as there seem to be employees prepping for tonight's guests. We barely get ten feet inside before we're stopped. A man who looks to be in his late twenties and is wearing a pair of cargo shorts that don't belong in this environment, whether it's closed or not, and a graphic T-shirt. He's maybe an inch or two shorter than Michael who steps toe to toe with him.

"We're closed; what do you want, my guy?" His piss poor attitude reminds me of the Situation circa season four of Jersey Shore.

I clear my throat and step into his line of sight. The shit head doesn't even acknowledge my presence.

"Hello, I'm here to speak with Matt." The tone of my voice is as sharp as a knife. The mystery man glares at me before he speaks.

"And, who the fuck are you?"

Michael grabs hold of the man by the throat as soon as he begins to move toward me.

"My name is Mr. Ludovico. I will not make my request a second time." My face is a mask of indifference as the man struggles to free himself from Michael. Once he's released from the strong grip the man steps back as if he's been hit. Good, the seriousness of my being here is beginning to sink in.

The large open space, which looks to be a dance floor during normal business hours, is starting to hold an audience that I neither need nor want.

"Sorry, dude, I'll grab him." He disappears down a hallway to the right of the entry.

I jerk my head in a silent acknowledgement to the employees who have gathered, and they take the hint to scatter. Several moments later, a bald heavyset man who appears to be older than me begins to approach where Michael and I stand. He's got on a similar pair of cargo shorts – does no one have respect for male fashion around here? Hell, even a JCPenney catalog has more fashion sense than these jackasses. At least he's got enough sense to wear a solid black Henley T-shirt.

"How may I help you, gentlemen?" The newest addition asks once he's standing before me.

My eyes dart to Michael who nods subtly confirming the identity of the person before me. I arch a brow at Matt, what a disrespectful dick.

"As I stated to your associate, my name is Mr. Ludovico. My grandfather, Frederico, was the backer for Mr. Barone, who just happened to provide me with your information as the primary supplier for the area." Nothing about my name seems to click for him, however Barone does, how interesting. Matt's face begins to flush as his expression morphs into one of irritation. "The thing is my grandfather died a few days ago, and I was unaware of this business arrangement. So, as you can understand, I have some questions."

Michael and I end up in the back office of the club, where we sit down with Matt for the next few hours to discuss what exactly his part is in the manufacturing and distribution of the drugs. It doesn't take long to determine he's just a pawn in the bigger picture. Nothing about this man screams intelligence. Unfortunately, I'll have to wait to deal with him once we have more information. Shutting shit down now would just lead to a war I'm not ready for.

"Thank you for your time; I'll be in touch." I cut him off mid-sentence and stand abruptly. Thankfully, Michael follows suit and keeps pace until we're outside where the sun is beginning to set. We walk side by side to the car, and I let myself into the back seat just as my phone dings with a text. I pull my phone out of my jacket pocket and tap the notification icon. I can feel my face heat as I read the message. Even if I've never met the Barone girl before, I feel a responsibility to her and everything inside me screams to end her fucking father as soon as possible.

Milo:

> She's secure and en route with me. It's worse than you could have imagined.

Chapter 7

Nina

As I step into the warm sunshine for the first time in my entire life, I take in the feeling of the openness around me now that I am outside of the place I've called my home for as long as I can remember. The heat beating down from the sky warms my skin, and I can't help the smile that spreads across my face. I look over my shoulder to find Milo, only a half-step away from me as we walk toward a large SUV. My feet stop on the sidewalk as I take in my surroundings. I hesitate before asking for something I've wanted to do for so long.

"Can I touch the grass?" My voice is so small as the question passes my lips. His eyes become glassy with unshed tears at my request. I'm sure it's an odd request. Who would want to touch grass? But I've never had the opportunity to even be outside, this is all so new to me.

"Of course, Nina." His reply comes across so much gentler than he was when speaking with my father.

My mouth forms into the widest grin that's ever graced my face. I take a few cautious steps toward the large plot of bright green lawn in front of the house. As I kneel down and press my hand against the blades of grass, which prickle my skin, I take in a sharp breath at the sensation. It's unlike anything I've ever felt before, and tears begin to well, stinging my eyes. I quickly lift my hand and wipe the moisture away before standing back up to face Milo.

"I'm ready." The words come out breathier than I mean for them to, yet with the emotion I'm feeling, I'm shocked that I can still find the words to speak at all. Once I'm seated in the large vehicle, Milo climbs in and sits next to me. It's not lost on me that he keeps his distance, which I'm more appreciative of than I can express at the moment. When the man behind the wheel finally begins to drive, Milo pulls out his phone and taps on the screen.

My gaze drifts to the window as we begin our trip. The outside world passes us by with every second we're on the road. I must confuse the men in the car when I gasp a few times because I feel both of their eyes land on me. I can't help my reaction. Everything is new, I've only seen the world like this through movies Cece has let me watch on TV.

A while later, we're making a left onto a long drive. Gorgeous rose bushes line the right side of the car and lead toward a huge building. My breathing begins to grow frantic as the realization of today's events hits me like a ton of bricks. The mansion - yes reader, you read that correctly. A fucking mansion - comes clearer into view with every second that passes, which doesn't help my emotions. Milo must sense the change within me because he turns toward me.

"Nina, I promise you. No one here will hurt you." The sincerity in his voice helps ease my nerves a little. "You will have the ability to explore, right now we just want to get you inside and the boss will explain why you're here. Ok?"

My eyes prick with unshed tears as I nod in response. Unsure of the proper procedure, I wait for Milo to let me out of the car once we're parked. A moment later the door opens and he extends a hand to help me step down. When I do, I'm greeted by a gorgeous older woman about the same age as Cece. Her dark hair is pulled back into a tight ponytail at the nape of her neck. Her eyes remind me of hot chocolate on a cold winter night. With a sharp jawline it makes her neck appear impossibly long yet, she looks perfect.

"Hi, Sweet Girl, my name is Giovanna Ludovico." She says as she approaches me and folds her arms around me in a tight squeeze. "You may call me Vanna if you'd like."

Milo clears his throat interrupting her, "Va – Mrs. Ludovico, don't overwhelm her."

She waves her hand at him in a gesture that says she'll do as she pleases and it makes me giggle. A sound that surprises the hell out of me. How am I so comfortable around these people?

"I'm Nina." I reply shyly; my voice is barely a whisper.

Giovanna wraps her surprisingly strong arm around my shoulder and guides me up the steps and into the large home. We're greeted by another woman once we're inside. She's about the same age, her blonde hair is styled in a short bob that somehow makes her slightly round face look a bit longer than it is.

"Nina, this is Mrs. Jade De Luca. She's our housekeeper and keeps our home in working order." Giovanna smiles as she introduces the woman standing in front of us.

"Hi, dear, you may call me Jade if you wish or Mrs. De Luca." She grins and glances toward Milo before continuing. "Or if you'd like, the boys like to call me Mrs. D. when I'm not around and think I don't know." She winks, and Milo stifles a laugh. "You should know by now, child, I know everything."

"Yes, ma'am." Milo snorts.

Mrs. De Luca – no I don't like that; it feels too formal – Jade steps toward me and extends a hand. When I lift mine to place in hers, she speaks quietly just to me.

"It's so nice to meet you, Nina. If you need anything, just shout. You'll be ok here, dear."

Jade disappears somewhere in the house as Giovanna and Milo lead me on a tour of the building. It's so big that they have a living room and a den, five bedrooms on either side of the house and on the second floor making a total of fifteen freaking bedrooms! Plus, Jade's got her own quarters so that she can be on call for anything the house may need during the night. My jaw is still on the floor back in the entry way as they explain all of this while they show me around. As we approach an open door on the second floor, Milo vanishes into a room that neither of them disclose anything about. She leads me into the open room and smiles brightly at me as I take in the surroundings. This bedroom is larger than the entire space I had at home.

"This will be your room." The warmth in her tone makes me feel so at peace. "Giovanni will want to see you soon, but he is finishing up with a situation that came up today."

"Who is Giovanni?" Curiosity fills my voice as the question passes my lips.

The door to my study opens without warning. I look up with my Glock in hand, aimed at the ready to shoot the fucker who entered without permission — until I see its Milo. Ok, he has a pass. I've been waiting for him. He looks completely drained from the day's events. As soon as my friend slides down to sit on the couch along the wall, I stand to grab us a couple of drinks. He lets out a breath when I hand over a heavy pour of the bourbon I've taken over since we got rid of Frederico. He had good taste in alcohol at least.

"You look like shit, run down what happened for me." I lift my own glass to my lips and take a long pull. The spicy liquid burns as it travels down my throat. Fuck, does it feel good after today.

Milo's shoulders lift and fall with another heavy sigh before he starts to explain what they found when picking up the girl.

"I thought it was fine at first; their house is nice. Not as big as this place, but not much can compare to this." He gestures around the room to make sure his point lands. "She had been locked away in a room on the second floor. It took up most of the floor so it felt like a studio apartment. But man, she had never been allowed outside of that room. She had never fucking touched grass until today. You should have seen the way she lit up when I let her feel it. Her smile is breathtaking. When we were on our way back here, I thought Danny Boy was going to crash with how often she would gasp when we passed something on the drive." He shakes his head dumbfounded, "She's in better shape than one would expect for being isolated for so long, but Jesus, I feel awful for the poor girl."

A rage begins to boil in my veins. When Barone made the comment he did about his daughter, I knew it couldn't have been a good situation, but fuck me. I may need to have a bit more fun with him than I did with Frederico. As if Milo can sense my thoughts he starts to speak again.

"I know you have a fuck ton on your plate with her dad and all that shit right now, but dude. We should talk about what happened the other night." Milo says with every bit of good intention.

I lift my head to face him before I continue.

"What is there to say? My dad was a good man who just so happened to marry into the mafia, and it was the worst decision he ever made for himself. I was still a kid when it happened. From what I remember, he and gramps had been fighting constantly because he wanted to move mom and me away from here. He wanted to get us out of this life. The next thing I know I'm slicing his throat after I was told the man had tried to take me away from my family." I take a deep breath and push forward, stopping mere inches away from him before I continue. "You will not tell her any of this. Understood?" He knows who I'm talking about. There is no need to add anything to my mother's stress in bringing me back into this life.

I don't bother to wait around for his response, instead I leave the study and walk the few doors down to where Nina will be staying when I hear my mother mention my given name.

"Giovanni will want to see you soon, but he is finishing up with some information that came in today."

I roll my eyes before I step into the doorway. I find my mother facing me and the woman I assume to be Nina with her back toward me. Her long dark strawberry blonde locks are hanging loose against her back. She looks tiny in stature, barely reaching five feet tall, so she appears to be drowning in an oversized matching sweatshirt and pants set.

"Who is Giovanni?" Her innocent question is filled with curiosity, and I don't actually hate the way it sounds coming from her.

"It's Johnny, actually." I announce as I walk in. Nina startles and lets out an adorable squeak as she whips around to face me. "I'm so sorry. I didn't mean to frighten you."

Now that the woman I've brought into my home is facing me, I can make out the way her grey eyes sparkle under the light. Flecks of a darker color highlight the outside of the iris. Her pouty lips part when she sees me for the first time. I can't help but grin when I notice the flush tinge her cheeks, the prettiest shade of pink. Her beauty is staggering.

"No, it's fine." The lie slips past her lips so effortlessly. "I'm not used to so many people being around."

I frown at her admission.

"How about we go into my study so we can talk? I'll explain every-thing." I offer an arm for her to take but she glances at my mom who nods her approval. "My mother can come with us, if you'd like."

Nina shakes her head as she steps gingerly toward me. She cocks a brow at my offered arm before linking hers with mine. She's noticeably stiff until I place my large hand on top of hers. We walk through the hall in silence and when we return to my study; I lead her to the same couch Milo had been sitting on earlier.

"Is it alright with you if I close the door?" The question may seem silly, but considering she's been locked behind closed doors her entire life, I will not lock her in without her consent.

Nina nods her head. The strawberry blonde hair falls around the front of her shoulders and frames her gorgeous face. The image of her hair wrapped in my hand while I fuck her from behind on this very couch pops into my mind. My cock stiffens at the thought, causing my slacks to become a bit more snug than I'd like for this conversation.

What the fuck, Johnny. She's never met a man besides her father until today. You can't go there. THIS. GIRL. IS. OFF. LIMITS.

I scold myself as I shake the thoughts from my mind and close the door before joining her on the couch. I take a seat the furthest away I can and offer her a genuine smile. Her grey eyes are locked on me as she waits for me to speak. I take a deep breath before I fill her in on everything that I can.

Chapter 9

Nina

A strong, warm, smooth yet gruff voice startles me. I spin on my heels to face the newcomer only to find the most beautiful man I've ever seen. Ok, shut up, I know I haven't seen many in real life, but even on TV or movies. The man that stands before me is the most stunning work of art mankind has to offer. His jawline is so sharp it could cut glass, and is covered in a short scruffy beard. His dark hair is slicked back against his scalp, making him look intimidating. Meanwhile, his milk chocolate-colored eyes, with flecks of gold that must sparkle like a Cullen in the sunlight, steal the breath from my lungs.

Feelings that make no sense rush to my core as I stare at the man. I follow dutifully as he guides me to a different room. We're sitting side by side on the couch, but he's seated so much further than anyone else has been since I was brought here this afternoon.

"Before I dive in fully, do you know anything about who I am? Or who your father is?" He keeps his eyes trained on mine, looking for something.

I blink rapidly at him, unsure what he's referring to.

"What do you mean? You're Giovanni and my dad is - well, my dad." As I reply, my mind whirls with confusion.

"Ok, Sweetheart." Giovanni's face twists in discomfort at the word. Meanwhile, his delicious voice has me in a chokehold, and I don't hate it. "There isn't an easy way to explain this, but I'm also not going to hide anything from you. I'm just going to dive in. I'm the new head of the Port Windsor Italian Mafia. My grandfather was my predecessor and he recently passed, which is how I met your father and found out about you."

I gasp at the revelation, "Like Scarface?" He cocks a brow at me with so much curiosity I can nearly see the questions forming in his mind. "What? When I finished all of my schooling when I was younger, Cece would bring out movies." I lift my shoulders in a shrug.

He shakes his head as a deep laugh rumbles through his chest.

"More like The Godfather, however – I won't allow drugs in my city." His words come out like ice.

"Okay," I drag out the word. "What does that have to do with my dad, Giovanni?"

He eyes me warily before continuing.

"Your father is one of the men who worked for my grandfather." He pauses for a moment while he stares into the depths of my soul. There's a clear hesitation when he opens his mouth to speak, but nothing comes out until after a few attempts. "I'm not sure how he came to be involved with the family, but that is something we're working on figuring out." Giovanni lets out a heavy sigh. "He told me this morning that he and my grandfather had an agreement in place to distribute drugs in Port Windsor."

"But I thought..?" I let the words die on my lips when I realized I interrupted him.

He chuckles and slides a little closer to me on the couch, patting my knee.

"You thought correctly. I won't allow drugs in my city, which is partially why you're here." His frustration is very clear as he speaks. "Your father admitted to some things that – what do you know about your mother?"

The sudden change of subject is jarring. My heart lurches in my chest at the mention of the woman who birthed me. I feel the tears begin to well in my eyes and wipe them away before they can fall.

"Dad refused to speak of her." My voice cracks as I confess, "I don't even know her name."

Giovanni stands abruptly, his hands balled into fists at his side. He's muttering under his breath as he paces back and forth in front of me a few times before returning to his position on the couch.

"Nina. I need you to know that you are safe here, and I will keep you safe for the rest of your life." He pauses as he waits for the words to sink in. When I nod acknowledging what he's said, he continues. "Your father murdered your mother when you were born because you weren't the bouncing baby boy he had hoped for."

My lungs fill as I breathe in a gasp.

"I don't understand. Why?" Tears begin to flow, falling freely down my cheeks.

The beautiful man in front of me shakes his head and drags his hand through his hair as he tries to figure out what he's going to say next.

"He didn't want anyone to know that you were still alive because you were a girl. This world can be extremely misogynistic and he kept you locked away this entire time because of that." A disgusted laugh erupts from his throat. "He admitted to Milo the only reason he had Cece care for you as thoroughly as she did was because he didn't want his reputation to be sullied with an –" Giovanni holds his hands up gesturing with air quotes, "idiot, even if she was a bitch."

My eyes are wide with shock and my veins run hot with boiling rage at his accusation. But I know deep in my soul, he's being truthful. Nothing about the way he's speaking to me or treating me feels like a lie. There is a respect here I've never felt with my father. With a shake of my head I glance back up at the man sitting next to me.

"Why did you want me here, Giovanni?" I ask the question that he hasn't yet answered.

"You know. I've threatened to shoot people for calling me Giovanni since I've been back." He drags a hand through his beard and shakes his head. I see a smirk in his eyes he's trying to hide behind his fingers. "Why don't I hate it when you call me that?"

Flutters explode in my belly with the way his eyes darken as he stares at me. I feel my cheeks flame and I quickly direct my focus to the floor. Oh look, there's a pretty hardwood floor in this room too. His fingers hook under my chin as he lifts my gaze back to his.

"What just happened? Where did you just go?"

I shake my head, unwilling to admit to myself, let alone him, that every fiber of my being feels like he belongs to me. I don't even understand the feelings I'm having. "No, nothing. I'm fine." I try to release myself from his hold but he won't let go.

"That's not how this is going to work, *Bella*. I won't lie to you, you're not going to hide from or lie to me. Understood?" His lips twitch as he tries to fight off a smirk but I can see the mischief in the way those milk chocolate eyes sparkle.

"I'm not lying!" I try to argue but the way he is staring has me rethinking and I let out a long breath. "I'm just overwhelmed by the way you're looking at me like you want to devour me or something, and I've never been around people, well, this many new people. This is all just so intense, am I going to be a prisoner here too? I mean, after all, it turns out that's all I was in my own home."

Johnny

A vortex of emotions emanates from the beautiful woman seated in front of me. Every part of me wants to pull Nina in and hold her close, but I know that's not what she needs. I lift her hand and clasp it between mine as I keep my eyes trained on her. She glances up at me through her thick lashes, tears stain her face from the onslaught of information I've thrown at her.

"Nina, you will never be a prisoner again." I squeeze her hands to offer some reassurance, and she lets out a breath. "You are free to go anywhere you wish. I just ask that you allow one of my men or myself to accompany you for your protection. At least until we know more about what my grandfather and your father got us sucked into." Her shoulders stiffen as I continue. "I wanted you here so that I can protect you from the evils of our world, and that is exactly what I intend to do." As soon as my explanation is complete she lets out a heavy sigh and her shoulders sag as understanding dawns on her of how serious I am about protecting her while allowing her freedom.

We sit in silence for a bit. When her tears continue, I stretch across the couch — my body hovers over hers while still holding her hand in one of mine. I grab the box of tissues that has Mrs. D written all over it since no one else would think to put them in here. After I pull a Kleenex free, the initial instinct to take care of her is so strong, yet I resist the pull and hand it over. She dries her eyes almost mechanically. I've never hated a man as much as I hate her father. Not even Andy, and my hate for him is the entire reason I'm in this situation.

"I don't want to push you tonight, but I need to know as much as you can tell me about your experience." Nina lifts her head to stare at me and I reach out to tuck a strand of hair behind her ear. She stills but doesn't pull away from my touch.

"What experience?" Her voice cracks as she speaks for the first time in a while.

My heart breaks for her. I'm terrified of what she's going to tell me. I'm worried that whatever it is will have me foregoing my current plan of gaining intel before I kill her father and just going to his house tonight to gut him like a fucking fish.

"Any and everything. The good, the bad, the ugly. Milo mentioned you had never been outside? I need to know everything." I pause when I see the tears begin to well again. "But for now, why don't we get you back to your room so you can get to bed. I'm sure you're exhausted"

I climb to my feet. Realizing our hands are still clasped together, I help her stand. She smiles shyly and then drops her hand from mine. My lips twitch as I try to stifle the grin her reaction to me causes. Gently placing my hand on the small of her back, I guide her out of my study and back to her room. The heat that radiates from her skin through the oversized sweatshirt has my dick stiffening in my pants, which I do my best to ignore. We pass Danny Boy in the hall, standing at attention outside of Nina's bedroom door. He nods to both of us and offers a kind smile to Nina. I stop at the doorway, not wanting to cross into her space. She turns to face me one last time.

"Giovanni," Nina's soft voice calls out to me. "Thank you for being honest with me. As much as I want to return the gesture and tell you everything…" the words die on her lips.

I start to move into her space but stop myself.

"*Bella*, you can tell me when you're ready. You're safe here. If you need anything, there is an intercom on your nightstand to reach out to Mrs. De Luca through the night." As I take a step back into the hallway, I notice one of my men leaning against the wall. "Danny Boy will be stationed outside of your room tonight if you need anything that Mrs. De Luca can't help with."

Nina nods and meanders into her bathroom, closing the door behind her. I turn to Danny who schools his facial expressions like the dutiful soldier he is.

"I'll be up for a bit if she needs anything." The words come across as more of a grunt than an actual statement.

A sharp throb in my temples wakes me from a restless sleep. When my eyes flutter open to see it's only four thirty in the morning, I groan loudly and curse under my breath. I throw the sheet off my legs and stand up to stretch my stiff muscles. *Fuck, I'm tired.*

I drag on a pair of dark sweatpants over my briefs and grab my phone from the nightstand before I make my way to the kitchen. My hand scrubs over my face as I try to drag myself out of sleep when I crash into something soft and warm that lets out an adorable little squeak. I drop both hands and reach out to steady whoever it is that I walked into, just to find a pair of sparkling silver eyes staring up at me. A small gasp escapes her when she realizes my hands are on her.

I cautiously take a step back and release her from my grip. That's when I realize she's only wearing a navy-blue sports bra and a pair of bike shorts. *FUCK. ME.* The matching sweatpants and shirt set gave no indication of just how tight her body is. Every bit of blood rushes straight to my groin. I already thought she was gorgeous, but Jesus Christ, that body and that face. Fuck, how did she get that lucky? How the fuck did I get this lucky? *No, damnit, Johnny. OFF. LIMITS.*

"Good morning, *Bella.*" My voice sounds like gravel from sleep.

Nina's cheeks flush a bright pink as I take her in.

"Morning, Giovanni," the soft cadence of her voice this morning is doing nothing for the erection, which is somehow now even harder after hearing her speak. "I hope I didn't wake you. I couldn't sleep and Danny said that there was a gym, and since I've never been in a gym I just wanted to see what you had." Her voice lowers to a whisper as she finishes speaking.

"*Fottuto Stronzo*," I growl at myself, and take a moment to fill my lungs with air as I allow myself to calm. "*Bella*, even if you were the reason I woke up, I couldn't be upset about that if it means you're the first face I see in the morning. But, no, you're not why I'm awake. Have you been there yet?"

Nina shakes her head gingerly. My lips twitch into a warm smile as I take her hand in mine. As we walk through the quiet halls of the Ludovico Estate, her presence brings a calm over me that I'm not used to. I feel her eyes on me while we walk. When I glance down at her, she tries to dart her gaze away which makes me chuckle.

"What is it, Short Stack?" A grin takes over my face and I don't try to hide it this time.

Oof, if looks could kill I'd be a dead man. She's got daggers in her eyes, and they're aimed directly at me.

"I liked *Bella*." Nina's sass slaps me right across the face. And I'm here for it.

Chapter 11
Nina

"Well, you're my Short Stack, *Bella*." Giovanni's response steals the air from my lungs. Why do I like that possessive reaction?

My cheeks heat as I allow the words to settle over me. A deep chuckle rumbles through his chest while we continue our walk through the house. It takes a few moments before I can find the right words. Being in his presence just does something to me that I can't explain. The organ in my chest thuds erratically as he gently squeezes my hand in an attempt to drag the answer from my lips.

"Why did you want me here? Why not just leave me with my dad? Why bother with a woman you've never met that obviously has more issues than Cosmopolitan?" My voice is so low as the embarrassment of my admission consumes me.

So many things rush through my mind as I wait for his answer, one that I realize he never actually disclosed last night. I keep my eyes focused on the ground as we continue to walk but he stops me. Giovanni's fingers grip my chin and drag my gaze up to meet his. The warmth in those milk chocolate irises is like a balm to my soul and eases some of the anxiety.

"Nina, the moment he told me that you were essentially being held like Rapunzel, there was no doubt that I had to get you out of there. No one should be held captive like that. Had I known of your existence sooner, I would have made it my fucking mission to get to you before I did." His thumb traces my bottom lip as he speaks, "Honestly, I wish I had gotten to you sooner, no matter how many issues you think you may have. I won't allow you to go through this life on your own any longer."

My lip's part with a gasp at his admission, his declaration. We don't speak again after that; Giovanni leads me into the home gym. My eyes go wide at the sheer mass of machines, I could work out every day for a month and never use the same device twice.

I must lose track of time because a light tap startles me from the weighted squat, causing me to drop the free weights which just narrowly miss my toe. Sweat drips down my brow as I take in Giovanni, now dressed in a dark grey suit that fits like a goddamn glove. *Holy shit, he's even more beautiful than I thought.*

"*Bella*, you've been in here for two hours." His tone is full of worry, but I see his lips twitch as he fights his reaction when I realize it's him. "Don't burn yourself out."

God damnit, I need to work on my face. It's so unfair that he can read me like this. I feel something pressed to my hand. When I look down, I notice he's handed me a towel. I smile and graciously accept, immediately wiping my face free from the evidence of my workout.

"Sorry, I got into what I was doing. I'm going to hate myself tomorrow." I groan, leaning down to grab the water bottle I've already refilled a handful of times.

"Go shower, Mrs. D will have breakfast ready for you when you get back to the kitchen." His tone is playful, but I can feel the command in his words. "I'll be out most of the day, go explore. I'll see you later, *Bella*."

Without another word, he walks out of the gym, leaving me on my own. I inwardly groan as I traipse behind in his wake and head back to my room. When I finally peel my workout gear off and step into the shower, a sense of peace settles over me. How is it that I never realized how little my own father cared about me? The affection shown from the people in this house is so wildly different from anything I've experienced in my sorry existence of a life thus far.

I step into the kitchen to find Jade rushing around working on a meal and Vanna seated at the kitchen island chatting away with a steaming mug in front of her. Vanna notices me first, her eyes crinkle in the corners as she smiles and waves me in to join her.

"Good morning, Sweetheart! I hear you're an early riser like my Giovanni." She murmurs.

Jade turns toward Vanna with a scowl on her face as she scolds, "Vanna, he's told you to call him Johnny how many times?"

Vanna rolls her eyes at Jade as I take a seat next to her. My cheeks flush at their conversation, realizing I've only been calling him Giovanni.

"What is it, Sweetheart?" Vanna pulls me in close, wrapping me in a side hug as she greets me.

I shake my head, not ready to unpack what him allowing me to call him that means. She squeezes me tighter against her side as she chuckles knowingly just as Jade directs her attention to me.

"Good morning, Nina! Would you like some coffee?" Her pleasant tone makes my lips turn into a bright grin.

"Oh, uh – I'm not allowed to have coffee." I admit, you could hear a pin drop at the silence that falls over the room.

Jade and Vanna share a look that shows concern mixed with fury. Jade leans across the counter and clasps my hands in hers.

"Unless you are allergic to something, you may have whatever you like." Her soft smile tugs at my already fragile emotions. "If I don't know how to make it, I'll figure it out or call in a professional chef."

My eyes begin to well with tears as Jade whips up the best breakfast I could ever hope for. When my confession of breakfast being a revolving door of yogurt with granola or fruit, she took it upon herself to create a smorgasbord of options for me to try. After tasting things such as eggs, bacon, pancakes, and a number of other breakfast menu items, I feel like my stomach will burst if I take another bite.

"Jade, I – you – this is too much." I push the plate away, "Everything is so good, but I –"

The words die on my lips as she snorts out a frustrated laugh.

"Oh, you poor girl, is this the first time you've been full?" I don't have a chance to respond when a group of men in suits begin to file into the kitchen. I think they're the same copy and paste ones from yesterday based on how a few of them stare. Jade turns her attention to the men, "Help yourself, boys, I'm not taking requests today."

Chapter 12
Nina

Today is the first day of the rest of my life. Yea, I know it's been said a million times. At least in the movies and books I've had access to. But for me, it's true.

As I step outside, greeted by the sun set high in the sky overhead, a lightness fills me that I'm not used to. The heat kisses my skin, making my bare arms and shoulders warm. A purple tank top that barely reaches my stomach is the only thing I could find from the dresser in my room after my shower.

I take a deep breath as I stroll deeper into the gardens behind Giovanni's home. Tears begin to flow as I take in so many new things at once; the ability to stop and smell a flower for the first time makes my heart stutter in my chest. The emotions are overwhelming as I appreciate every new experience. I don't think I'll ever fully understand why my father kept me locked away, but it landed me here. In a house where, after half a day, I feel more at ease than I ever felt at what I thought was my home.

Abel, the man that took over as my shadow for Danny, follows closely behind, not allowing me out of his sight. I glance over my shoulder to see him hovering a few yards away. No matter how far I walk, he's always right there. You'd think after being locked away for my entire life, someone tailing me everywhere I go would be a bother. Honestly, I find it more comforting than anything. I don't know anything about the outside world, and that security blanket makes me feel safe.

A throat clears from behind me and I turn to see Abel standing a little closer than he had been with a hesitancy I didn't expect from a big, bad mafia man. Maybe I've seen too many movies?

"Ms. Barone, I was instructed to remind you by Mrs. De Luca to re-apply your sunblock." Abel's voice seems strained as he hands me the bottle of lotion.

"Please, Abel. Call me Nina." I reply and take the bottle of lotion in my hand as I continue to where a tree sits, more secluded than the rest of the gardens. I take a seat under the protective shade of the branches before I generously rub more sunscreen into my skin until the product is fully absorbed. My mind, even if I feel more at ease here, it is a chaotic maze of what if's and why's, that I can't seem to wrap my head around. I lean my head against the trunk of the tree and close my eyes for a few moments, trying to clear the unknowns.

My eyes flutter open to see the sun is further west in the sky than when I closed them. I must have dozed off. Anxiety begins to seep into my bones, why did Abel not wake me? Suddenly, a calm washes over me when I feel warmth radiating against the right side of my body. When I glance over to find Giovanni with a laptop on his legs, I'm not surprised in the least.

"How long have I been out?" I ask, my voice is scratchy with sleep.

Giovanni closes the computer screen before he responds.

"A few hours." He admits, "I called to check on you and told Abel to let you sleep since you were up so early. He just left you about twenty minutes ago when I sat down." Giovanni stands to his feet and holds his hand out for me to join him, which I do.

I glance around to find no one else is near. My cheeks heat under his watchful gaze as I take his outstretched hand. He pulls me to my feet a little harder than I expected, which lands me flush against his solid chest. The air rushes from my lungs and I step back, pressing against the hard wall of warm muscle. My hands linger along the ripple of his firm abs while our eyes are locked on one another.

"Hi, Short Stack." Giovanni's lips curve into a wide grin as he takes in my confused state. "How was your day of exploration?"

My eyes dart around our surroundings, seeing all the greenery and plants in the early evening light and I can't help the emotion that wells in my chest. I quickly drop my gaze to my feet and let out a soft sigh, unable to articulate just how meaningful today was for me. Even if I wasn't entirely alone, the freedom to walk around outside isn't something I ever thought I'd be able to do.

"Nina?" The smooth gruffness of his voice wraps around me like a blanket of calm. "Do you want to talk about it?"

My eyes roll into the back of my head so dramatically it would make Regina George proud. *Do I want to talk about it?*

"Even if I could figure out where to start, I don't know what to say. My entire world has been turned upside down, and while I'm thankful for that and for your part in that…" the sentiment dies on my lips. What could I say that would express my thanks and not come across as sarcastic? "Giovanni, I – I am thankful for you. I just –" I groan as my gaze darts up to his. The golden specks sparkle under the evening sun so beautifully it's hypnotic. "Truth, right?"

"Always, *Bella*." He nods in agreement and makes himself comfortable, leaning against the tree trunk while I allow my mind to assemble the correct words.

"I'm scared. Apparently, my defense mechanism is sarcasm. Who would have thought someone locked away from the world could develop a sarcastic personality? Well, leave it to me." I bury my face in my hands for a moment, releasing a scream that has been building up since everything came to light last night. "I am thankful for you, for everything. But, I'm so used to being beaten or worse if I don't control that flaw. I'm afraid that even telling you this much will have me locked away without food for a day or two. I don't want to go back to that."

Johnny's body stiffens next to me which only makes me flinch as I prepare for impact. *Crap, I should have stayed quiet.*

Chapter 13
Johnny

Anger radiates off me in waves as her words fully register. I take deep breaths while I attempt to center myself. The calming techniques I've learned over the years aren't doing shit for me right now though.

"*Bella*, I swear to all hell, the next time I see your father," I growl through gritted teeth. "I'm going to take a knife and slit him from groin to sternum for what he's done to you."

Nina's breath hitches in a way that doesn't express fear, but interest. I suppress a grin, the look on her face tells me she doesn't understand the emotional response. Not that I'd expect her to, given the circumstances of her upbringing and how she's come to be here. However, it gives me hope for what's to come. Or at least what I hope is to come. With my hand pressed gently on the small of her back, I continue leading her back inside to where my mother and Mrs. De Luca are sitting at the kitchen island waiting for us.

Mrs. D's expression becomes feral when she takes in the gorgeous woman beside me. I glance over, my gaze dragging from the top of her head down to her toes. I don't notice anything obvious; her cheeks are a little flushed from the day in the sun but – then it hits me.

"Damnit Abel! I told you to make sure she reapplies sunblock! Look at her porcelain skin, it's as red as a freshly steamed lobster!" Mrs. De Luca yells at the soldier assigned to guard Nina today.

The kid's face drains of color which makes me chuckle. You don't want to be on Mrs. D's bad side. Nina turns to face me with an unspoken question on the tip of her tongue as she raises her fingers to touch her face. She definitely has that sun kissed look about her and damn, does it look good on her.

"I don't understand," Nina's eyes dart between my mom and Mrs. D who looks like she's ready to strangle Abel.

He steps forward with his shoulders pushed back and standing at his full height as he approaches me, ready to accept whatever punishment I deem appropriate. It takes every bit of self-control to keep my laughter at bay.

"Ms. Barone, I'm so sorry. I should have been more aware of the situation." He eyes Nina a bit longer than necessary, and I step between them wrapping an arm around her waist, staking my claim.

"Please, Abel. I told you earlier, it's Nina." She lets out a frustrated sigh which makes Abel eye me for approval.

"Relax, I'm not going to kill you, kid. Just stay diligent." My arm wraps a bit tighter around Nina's waist before I continue. "But if you look at her that way again, not just as your charge during a protection detail, I will fuck you up. Understood?"

My mother's chuckle pulls my attention from Abel, who takes that moment to disappear from the room. A mischievous glint in her eyes has me cocking a brow in her direction. She ignores me, as only a mother could when she doesn't want to share her thoughts, and stands to pull Nina to the kitchen island where Mrs. D already has a meal waiting.

It amuses me that the two of them dote on her like their own long-lost child. When Nina is finally comfortable with more than a few people being around her at one time, they're going to spoil the fuck out of her. I can already feel it.

"Child, if you don't take a seat as well and eat some dinner, I will make sure you don't get a cinnamon bun for a week." Mrs. De Luca scolds me from where she stands, pushing a plate toward an empty chair. The way her eyes are gleaming in the light tells me not to test her.

"You do realize you're ordering around the Capo, correct?" I ask as I try and fail to stifle my laughter.

"You are still the sweet boy I helped raise so, take a seat. You need to eat too." Mrs. De Luca waves her hand in the direction of where she wants me. "Don't argue with your elders, Capo or not."

"Yes ma'am," I meander over to the open spot and slide into position on the other side of Nina. "Just don't order me around in front of the others, it will ruin my street cred or something like that." I tease.

My mother scoffs and smacks me upside the head, "Giovanni, you already know every man who walks through the front door would drop to their knees if any one of the women in this house asked them to. You may be the Capo, but *we* hold the power." She leans in close so that I'm the only one who can hear and continues quietly. "She already has more strength than she realizes. Just wait until Nina finds her voice, she will be unstoppable."

The Caprese Chicken Saltimbocca that Mrs. De Luca made is delicious, the blend of herbs, spices, and vinegar plus the prosciutto is my version of a comfort meal. Fuck, you can't go wrong with prosciutto. When my eyes land on Nina after thirty minutes of keeping my gaze trained anywhere but at her, I feel a punch in the gut. Her eyes are filled with tears.

"*Bella.* What is it?" I ask as I stand and position myself next to her. I grip her chin like I have before and tip her face up so that she can see my eyes. Her lack of trust may be absolutely warranted, but damn, I hate it. "Talk to me, Nina." I order.

Her shoulders sag at the command and she closes her eyes, so she doesn't have to look at me.

"You said something when we were on our way in here that's been bothering me." Her chest begins to lift and fall rapidly as she tries to piece her thoughts together. "You said you want to kill my dad."

"And I will," I confirm, her eyes are still closed as she continues.

"That confession should scare me, but it doesn't. It excites me. Why does it excite me?" She questions, as a single tear falls down her cheek.

Chapter 14
Nina

It's been a week since Giovanni's men came for me and brought me here. A week since I last saw my father or the woman who raised me. You'd think I'd be devastated that I haven't seen the only two people who have been in my life since I was born. If I'm honest, the only thoughts I've had of them are just how serious Giovanni was about killing my dad. What does that say about me?

My mornings are much the same as that first day here, I start out in the gym and then am practically force fed by Jade. Who am I kidding, I love it. She's given me more love and affection in the last week than I've had from anyone in my life up to this point. I've been trying new foods daily, though I've learned my limits and don't overeat. My afternoons are spent in the garden, much like today.

The sun is hiding behind the clouds which has the sky a shade of grey. I pull on the hoodie that was on my bed this morning when I woke up with a note from Giovanni.

My lips twitch at the corner as I wrap my arms around myself. The shirt smells like him, a warm sweet spice. I recognize the cinnamon from the revolving oven door of cinnamon rolls that Jade makes every day, but there's something else, a hint of fruit. I melt into the scent a little more and I cop a squat under my favorite tree. The cool breeze feels wonderful on my face as I lean my head back and close my eyes. This is my favorite part of the day.

A vibration on my legs startles me and my eyes flutter open as I glance down to see a long hair, tortoise tabby cat purring away in my lap. My lips part with a gasp as the sweet ball of fluff opens its eyes and stares up at me.

"Well, hello you. Where on earth did you come from?" I ask as I cautiously drag my fingers through its silky fur. It's a cat, obviously it doesn't answer me, but the animal is staring at me as if it knows exactly what I'm saying.

When I raise my gaze, I find Danny and Abel are speaking with their backs toward me. The cat stands on my legs and climbs up my chest to pat my cheek with its paw to drag my attention back down to it. I can't help but smile at the needy animal.

"Aren't you the sweetest thing; do you have a name?" I ask the question out loud as I feel around its neck for a collar. The poor animal has no form of identification, when it flops over onto its back, I get an eye full, confirming its gender is male. Wow this cat has got a set on him.

A snap from a few feet away pulls my attention back up to find Giovanni walking toward me with a frown pulling at his lips. He stops at my feet, looming over me.

"You've been out here so long you've been adopted by a cat?" He cocks a brow at me as he takes in the fur ball in my lap.

I giggle, a sound I've only made once before. His face relaxes into a wide grin at my reaction to his comment. He looks so free when he smiles like this.

"I don't know what that means," I admit as I pull the cat to my chest for a squeeze before laying him on the soft lawn. I take Giovanni's outstretched hand. He pulls me to my feet with a wide smile on his face as he loops his arm around my waist and holds me tight against his chest. My stomach twists with a fluttery feeling inside at the connection between us. This reaction seems to be happening more with each passing day. "How was your day?" I ask, trying to ignore my body's response to him.

We take a few steps to find the cat following us. He keeps pace with us and refuses to lose his sight of me. Giovanni chuckles and shakes his head as he releases me to pull out his phone. He taps a few times on the screen before bringing it to his ear. After a few seconds someone must answer because he starts speaking.

"Go get a few litter boxes to put around the house, cat food, dishes, treats and litter, obviously." He pauses and his eyes darken as he listens to whomever is on the other end of the call. "Did I ask for your opinion? No, go get the stuff and be back within the hour or I'll shoot you in the foot. Got it?" His response comes out in a snarl, and he hangs up, sliding the phone back into his jacket pocket before we step inside. My eyes dart between him and the cat several times before he explains what just happened.

"It's called the cat distribution system. I've heard of it, but never seen it in action. That cat is yours now, Short Stack." He leans down and drags his fingers through the cat's fur. "What are you going to name it?"

With my mouth agape, I stare up at him with question after question rapid firing through my mind. I feel the warmth of fur wrap around my leg as the cat, *my* cat, weaves between to capture my attention. My eyes begin to well with tears and I launch myself at the man who has become a pillar in my life in such a short amount of time. My arms fold tightly around his muscular middle as I take in the familiar scent. Tears begin to fall, and my shoulders begin to shake as I sob against this beautiful man. He wraps himself around me like a snake strangling its prey, but this is protective and maybe just a little possessive.

Chapter 15
Johnny

A shrill scream and yowl jolt me out of an already restless sleep. I untangle myself from the covers and throw them off my body as I leap out of bed, remembering to grab the Glock from under my pillow. My feet pad hard against the smooth hardwood floor as I run in the direction of the noise. As I quickly rush toward Nina's room, the screams and yowls become louder and masculine grunts become clearer.

Fury begins to pump through my veins, I slam my body into the bedroom door and it splinters before crashing to the floor. Her cat, which she still has yet to name, is clinging on to the back of an intruder. The nails of his front paws are digging into the man's shoulder while her cat uses its hind legs to scratch the hell out of the intruder's back. *Good kitty.* Nina is hanging over the man's shoulder, repeatedly punching his back, which isn't even doing so much as to make the man flinch.

"Put her the fuck down," I snarl at the man who stiffens. Nina's eyes find mine; she has tears streaming down her face, a mixture of fear and anger etched across her face.

When he stands to his full height, I catch sight of the bald head with a very distinct tattoo on the side of his skull. I realize it's one of the men that have been hanging around with Mr. Barone. Interesting. His lips turn into a malicious grin as he slides her down the front of his body. The cat is still clawing his back as he climbs up to the man's shoulder and sinks his teeth into the balding head. Barone's man jerks and ends up tossing the cat onto the floor. I hear Nina's scream as I raise the gun, my hand tightens around the grip as I aim at the man's head and squeeze the trigger. A loud shot rings through the room as Nina scrambles across the space to reach the fur ball.

Don't fuck with my woman or her cat.

I shove the gun into the back of my briefs, the mixture of heat from the recent discharge and coolness of the metal causes a strange sensation. My feet are moving at their own accord to reach Nina and *Pinhead*. She's curled over top of him protectively. When I pull her onto my lap, I see the cat is sitting on his haunches licking his fur clean. Of course he wouldn't be phased by taking on a mobster. Fucking fur ball.

"*Bella?* Short Stack, can you look at me?" I whisper just as Milo and Danny enter the room. Nina ignores my request and buries her face in my chest, not looking up.

"Holy fuck." Milo's shock echoes through the room as he takes in the scene before us.

"Where the fuck were you?" I stand, pulling Nina up with me as I cradle her to my chest. "You are supposed to guard for her at night. So, explain to me exactly how the fuck this happened."

As I approach Milo and Danny, Nina whimpers for her cat. I glare at Danny before I turn to set Nina on her feet. Gently cupping her cheeks between my palms, I stare into the depth of her baby greys before I speak.

"Get Pinhead and gather whatever you'll need for the morning. You're staying with me in my room from now on." The words come out as a whispered command but her small nod in response relieves some of the adrenaline still pumping through my veins. I turn back toward my men while my hands are still on her cheeks to keep her in place, "Cover the body, she doesn't need to see this."

Danny is the one to move, swiftly pulling a sheet from Nina's bed and draping it over the bald intruder. Once he's covered, I release her to do as I asked.

I usher my men into the hall and before another word is uttered my hand is wrapped around Danny's throat. With a quick step forward, I slam his large frame against the wall. His eyes remain calm as Milo steps in beside me.

"Johnny, I pulled him this afternoon because I needed someone who understands the severity of the situation to do surveillance down at one of Barone's properties." Milo explains, "Michael and I assigned Rich to Nina tonight."

I drag my eyes from Danny to take in my friend. Milo's sincere expression has me lowering Danny who begins to cough as he attempts to catch his breath.

"Where the fuck is Rich then?" I snarl at Milo.

"I'll have Michael review the security footage and let you know as soon as I have that information." Milo slides his phone from his suit. He taps a handful of times on the screen before returning the phone to the inside jacket pocket. "He's taking care of it now."

Nina steps out of the bedroom with Pinhead cuddled tightly to her chest. Her strawberry blonde hair is now pulled into a tight bun. Her shoulders relax when she sees that I'm still standing there. I extend my hand for her to join us, which she does. Her tiny body fits perfectly against mine.

"Sir, what would you like us to do with the body?" Danny is the one who speaks this time.

My chest rises and falls with a heavy exhale before I speak. "Check him for any ID, however I recognized the skull tattoo. He's one of Barone's. See what you can find and then dismember the body and have the pieces delivered to all of Barone's known hangouts." Nina tilts her face up to look at me with a question in her eyes.

"Why would my dad have someone try to take me like this?" Her voice is shaky as she asks the question. "I don't understand why he suddenly cares enough about me or where I am when he essentially sold me to you."

My arm tightens around her shoulders, and I press my lips to her hair, inhaling the soft scent of lavender. She melts further into me, if that's even possible.

"*Bella*, that is exactly what I'm going to find out."

Nina's nod is full of frustration and annoyance. I can see the rage in her eyes. When my gaze returns to Milo, he jerks his head toward Danny who takes the gesture as it's meant, and they both walk into the bedroom for the body.

"Thanks, Johnny." She shakes her head with her nose scrunched up in a look of disgust, "No, I don't like that. Giovanni suits you."

My shoulders shake with laughter as I lead her into my room, Pinhead still held tight to her chest. *Lucky fucker.*

"Fortunately for you, I enjoy the sound of that name on your lips." I reply, my voice full of innuendo. Nina's face turns a shade of pink I've only ever seen on the color wheel, and my God, is it gorgeous on her skin.

When we finally reach my room, I guide her inside and she turns to face me, her lips turned downward in a frown.

"Why did you call him Pinhead?"

Chapter 16

Nina

"Why did you call him Pinhead?" My voice is shaky as I ask the question. My body is still trembling as I try to wrap my mind around what just happened. Someone just tried to abduct me out of my bed.

"He sunk his nails and teeth into that man like he was a pincushion." Giovanni shrugs. "It felt appropriate, given the circumstances."

I shake my head at his reasoning, my lips curving upward no matter how hard I try to fight the amusement. Giovanni pulls me flush against him again. The feel of his bare chiseled physique against my body sends an unfamiliar warmth to my belly.

"This is a loaded question, but I've got to ask. Are you ok?" He pulls away to stare down at me. His brown eyes stare into my soul as he waits for me to respond.

I choke on a laugh. "I shouldn't be. Maybe I won't be tomorrow, but right now..." My shoulders lift and fall dramatically with a shrug. "Right now, I'm oddly comforted by the fact that you didn't hesitate to do what you did."

Giovanni nods his head in understanding, then lets out a sigh.

"Nina, can you tell me everything that happened?" The words come across much softer than he's spoken since I was pulled from my bed. A soft knock sounds at the door and Pinhead leaps from my arms. He crosses the room so quickly it's a blur of fur until he's on his hind legs hissing at the doorknob. Yea, that name is totally going to stick.

"Psp psp psp, come here, Pinhead, it's ok." I call out for my fur covered protector, "Giovanni won't let anyone hurt me. We're safe in here, kitty." He rushes over to me but looks over his little shoulder at the man I promised would keep us safe, like he's unsure. *Dude, he just shot a man to protect us. I think we're good.* If only a cat could read my thoughts.

"Should I be afraid to fall asleep with him in here?" Giovanni asks half teasingly as he twists the door handle and pulls the door open toward him to show Jade with a look of concern on her face and the litter box from my room. Crap, I knew I was forgetting something.

The two of them have a hushed conversation that I can't make out, so I turn around. My bare feet pad against the smooth hardwood floor as I approach the enormous bed. Damn, this thing is bigger than the one I was sleeping in. This bed is set a little higher than the one in my room, so I have to jump a little to get on to the mattress. Pinhead leaps up next to me and sniffs around as I take a seat, my legs crisscrossed under me as I wait for Giovanni to return.

"Get some rest, sweet girl, I'll have a cinnamon bun ready for you tomorrow with a hot chocolate." Jade calls past the opening as she shoves the litter box into Giovanni's chest. "Don't make her talk if she's not ready, Johnny." He rolls his eyes and closes the door behind her retreating form. He disappears into the connected bathroom where he must leave the litter box because it's no longer in his hands when he returns.

My eyes roam along the ridges and valleys of his muscular tattoo covered chest as he closes the distance between us. I've never seen such a beautiful human in my life, not even on TV. My cheeks flush when I realize he's standing directly in front of me. I glance up to find him grinning down at me, but he doesn't call me out for my ogling.

"Ok, *Bella.* Do you think you can tell me what happened?" He repeats the earlier question from before Jade arrived.

I blow out a long breath and stare down at my hands, laying on my crossed legs.

"I was asleep, so I don't remember much. I remember feeling as if I were floating and then my chest suddenly crashed into something hard which stole the air from my lungs. That's what made me open my eyes.

When I did, I was staring at a back." My chest heaves as I fight back a sob. "He made a comment that I belonged to the Barone family and –" my eyes close tight as I try to fight off the memory. I don't want to say the last part.

"Go on." Giovanni's kind voice is closer as I feel the bed dip next to me. His body is so much closer to me now. The warmth radiating from his skin sends a jolt of electricity through me, making me shiver.

"I – I don't want to say it." I admit and turn to face him, my eyes shine with unshed tears. He presses his palm to my cheek, and I press into the connection.

"It's ok, *Amore*. You can tell me anything." The confidence in his words should provide comfort, but the words I have to say have me more frightened than when I was pulled out of my home to come here.

I close my eyes again, savoring the warmth of his hand against my skin for just a moment before I speak.

"He said that even if I wasn't the heir that my dad wanted, he could use me for leverage and payment to have you taken care of."

Giovanni mumbles a curse under his breath. He takes my face between his hands and. presses his lips to my forehead. I suck in a sharp breath at the connection, my eyes flutter open to take in the man before me.

"Is there anything else?" I shake my head slowly, afraid to move and feeling vulnerable in this position. "I'll be back in a few minutes, ok?"

"Sure," It's only a single word, but when it passes my lips it sounds breathy and full of desire.

I stare back at my hands as he rushes out of the room and hollers through the hall for someone to stand by. My mind reels from the events of the past few hours. Unsure of what's going to come next, I crawl to the top of the bed and rest my back against the pillows on the side that look like it hasn't been slept on. Pinhead follows close behind. He mewls when I pull my knees to my chest and curls into a ball next to me. My heart aches at the thought of something happening to Giovanni because of me. I need to help, somehow.

I'm not sure how long it's been when the door slowly cracks open with a soft creek as Giovanni steps back inside. His eyes look as exhausted as I feel. When he realizes I'm still awake, he stops suddenly.

"I'm sorry, Short Stack; did I wake you?" He crosses the room and climbs onto the mattress with ease. Damn him and those long man legs.

I shake my head no and scoot myself down under the covers. Pinhead stands and stretches before he migrates to the foot of the bed when Giovanni covers himself from the waist down with the sheet.

"Get some rest, *Bella*. We will talk more tomorrow."

Chapter 17
Johnny

A light lavender scent cuts through the haze of a very vivid dream. An overwhelming warmth coats my skin, something heavy weighing me down. My eyes flutter open and I tense, my mind still in that fog between sleep and consciousness. Reaching for my Glock under my pillow, I pause when a wild mess of strawberry blonde hair comes into view. The woman the halo of reddish gold belongs to, sprawls across my chest.

Her soft breasts are pressed against the rippling muscles that I work so hard for. Her thin T-shirt is the only thing separating our bare skin. The hard peaks of her soft breasts press into me despite the flimsy excuse of her night clothes. My cock throbs as it strains against the black boxer briefs hidden under a pair of dark sweats I had the forethought to wear to sleep. Nina's head and that riot of curls blocks my line of sight, but if I could see past her head, I'm sure the thick grey material would be stretched toward the ceiling, tented over my throbbing dick. She's gonna fucking freak. And not just because the monster in my pants was roused, but because we're pressed together without her knowledge or consent.

My heart pounds erratically in my chest while trying to calm the flow of blood to my groin so she's at least not confronted with my raging hard-on. All progress is thrown out the window when she stirs and lets out the sweetest noise. Jesus fuck, that little moan is going to be the star of every wet dream I have going forward for the rest of my life.

Nina's body goes rigid as her eyelids flutter open, her long lashes tickling my chest. She scrambles off of me and backs away to the other side of the bed, narrowly missing Pinhead who's asleep on her pillow. I rush to cover myself with my own pillow to try to hide the evidence of not only my morning wood, but what she does to me.

"Giovanni?" The first word out of her mouth is my name and hell, does it sound good with that morning rasp. I wonder if she'd sound like that if I woke her up with my face buried between her thighs. I curl my lips inward as I suppress the grin that my dirty thoughts are causing.

"Morning, Short Stack." I greet the gorgeous woman in my bed. "Are you ok? I'm not sure how we ended up in an aggressive cuddle, but I can sleep on the floor tonight if that would make you more comfortable." I scold myself for making the offer. There is nothing more I want than to wake up with her on me like that again. Well, ok maybe one thing, but obviously that's not happening any time soon.

Nina pulls the covers up over her chest to hide from me. She shakes her head and drags her hands over her face to scrub the sleep from her eyes. When she looks back up at me, she has a look of fear etched across her gorgeous features that makes my heart sink.

"I'm sorry. I didn't mean to." She rushes out, her voice trembles as she speaks. "I don't know what happened, I was over here when I fell asleep. Usually, I don't move when I sleep, I'm so sorry." She apologizes again.

I smirk up at her, unable to hide the amusement at her reason for worry.

"*Bella*, if I could wake up with you sprawled across my chest like that for the rest of my life, I will die a happy man. You did nothing wrong." I shake my head, trying to stifle the chuckle. "Answer me this. How did you sleep?"

Nina's breath hitches as she takes a moment to let the question sink in. Her features soften and that sweet pretty pink color tinges her cheeks again. As her body begins to relax, she lets the blanket lower. The hardened peaks of her soft breasts are still obvious through the thin material, and it takes all my willpower not to keep my eyes locked on them.

"I slept," her shoulders lift and drop as she lets out a heavy sigh. "Really well. I don't know that I've ever slept through the night like that." Her confession does nothing to help the aching need currently throbbing under the pillow I've still got over my cock.

I chuckle and throw my legs off the side of the bed and then toss the pillow at Nina which makes her squeal. When I stand, my hand immediately goes to adjust my dick. Even with the monster tucked between the waistband and my stomach, there is an undeniable bulge, which I'm not sure she's ready for.

"Go get some breakfast, Short Stack." My desire for her can't overshadow what I need to do today. "I need to get a shower before I head out for the day."

My bare feet pad across the smooth hardwood floor as I make my way into my bathroom. I go through the motions of turning on the shower. When I finally kick off the pants and boxer briefs, a groan escapes my lips. An instant relief when my cock springs free from the tight confinement.

God damn, I am fucked. Why do I only seem to get hard-ons for the ones that are off limits? As I step into the shower, the warm water pelts against my skin. I lean forward against the cool tile, my head rests against my forearm as my dominant hand wraps around the base of my still aching dick. My lips part in a deep groan as I squeeze, tightening my grip. I begin to slide my hand up and down my length, toying with the Jacob's ladder piercings while grazing my thumb over the top, swiping drops of pre-cum across the head of my dick.

My eyes close and I envision Nina spread out before me, burying my face between her thighs for as long as she can handle. As much as I want to take every first she'll allow, I know she's nowhere near ready to take me. I feel like a fucking monster having the feelings I do when she's got no experience with anyone, really, let alone the opposite sex. I let out a tortured moan as I pump my length only a handful of times before the telltale sign of a climax begins with tingling at the base of my spine. The fact that I'm so quick to find my release only confirms how fucked I am in this scenario. My balls begin to tighten, and I thrust my hips into my hand and curse as I paint the walls with my seed. Fuck.

After I finish cleaning up myself and the wall in the shower, I step out into the warm bathroom. I wrap a large towel around my waist and walk to the bathroom door. As soon as I pull the door open to my bedroom, I see Nina walking in with a mug of coffee and cinnamon roll. She's still dressed in the same flimsy sleep clothes she was in when I got into the shower. Her eyes go wide when she sees me. I cock a brow at her, my lips pulled into a tight grin, unable to hide my amusement.

"Hi, sorry. Um," she murmurs as she takes a few cautious steps toward me. "Jade asked me to bring these to you since you are going to be in a rush. I didn't realize – I didn't mean to – I'm so sorry for intruding." She stumbles over her words. That beautiful color stains her cheeks yet again.

I take a step toward her, closing the distance between us and grip her chin as I raise her gaze to mine. She's worrying her bottom lip as her eyes dart in any direction that isn't my eyes.

"Short Stack, look at me." She fights the command for only a moment before she's locked in on me. She swallows hard when I release her chin and caress the smooth skin that covers her cheeks before I continue. "*Amore*, you have nothing to apologize for. This is your room now too."

Her bright smile in response is the sweetest thing I've ever seen. When Nina steps out, she begins to close the door behind her, but I don't miss the fact that she glances back for one last look before she pulls it shut. My shoulders shake with silent laughter. I send a message asking that Abel and Rand, Nina's day protection, come to my room.

A quick loud knock sounds at the door a few moments later as I zip up my dark grey slacks.

"Come in." My voice sounds calmer than I feel. I pull a black button up shirt on as the heavy wood door slowly opens. "Get in here, there are some things we need to discuss." The two men step before me, dressed in matching suits, and stand with their hands clasped in front of them as they wait for my instruction. Abel's back is straight. The kid has become fond of Nina over the past week. I trust that he won't fuck up. After all, he nearly pissed himself when she got a sunburn. "The two of you have been briefed on what happened last night?" I don't wait for them to respond before I continue. "The two of you will shadow Nina from here on out. If anything happens to her, even something as simple as a hair on her head being out of place because you weren't doing your fucking job. I will make you wish for death as I peel the skin from your bodies while you watch, *capisci*?"

Milo and Michael are waiting at the door of my study as I approach. I nod in greeting and open the door. The two of them follow me in and take a seat at the chairs in front of my desk. When I take my place at the large chair behind my desk, my eyes dart between the two. While I trust these men with my life, someone fucked up and I want to know who.

"Speak." I bark out the command.

Michael sits up straighter in his seat and begins to speak, "We were able to identify the intruder as Bastian Caprioni. The security feed shows that Rich fell asleep next to her door. Caprioni moved Rich into her bathroom and jammed the lock so that he couldn't get out. He was still asleep when we found him."

I sit with my hands crossed in front of me at my desk. My foot taps quietly under the large piece of furniture as I wait for the information on how the hell Caprioni got in to begin with. Michael must sense my impatience because he clears his throat and finally delves into that portion of the story.

"From what we're able to determine, the man was able to get in through a blind spot. We have men rotating around the house every hour, however, the cameras are on a constant sweep, so during a rotation he must have gotten in." Michael's words sink in and the anger I felt last night is nothing in comparison to right now.

"You're telling me, that my grandfather, the motherfucker into drugs and behind a whole host of murders in his time as Capo, let a fuck up of this magnitude occur. A blind spot in security of this magnitude was not a simple oversight." My words come out in a roar that would make Mufasa tremble.

Michaels mask of calm flickers briefly before he puts it back in place. "When we looked back on the recordings, it seems he changed the angles and guard shifts about a week after you were set to come home."

Knowing that Frederico's involvement in the day to day wasn't quite as extensive as it is now, gives me reason to pause.

"So, someone told him I was coming home, and he knew he wouldn't be around for much longer." I chuckle darkly. An audible pop sounds in the room as I roll my neck, the tension from the last twelve hours taking a toll on my body. "Keep Rich in the cell downstairs. I'll deal with him later. Right now, I need you," my eyes lock on Milo who sits up straighter now that he has my attention. "We're going to make a scene and make sure Barone knows I'm not to be fucked with".

Milo's eyes gleam with mischief as my meaning clicks. His mouth twists into a wide grin as he jerks his head with a quick nod.

An hour later, once Milo's task is completed, the three of us are in one of the large SUVs with tinted windows heading to a familiar location. I pay no attention to the scenery during the drive, instead I drag my phone out of my jacket pocket and send a quick message.

Johnny:

> Short Stack, would you like to go out this evening?

I know she hasn't received the phone yet, but that message being the first thing she sees when she opens the box makes my smile widen.

The rest of the drive goes by quickly. When we pull into the parking lot, Michael, Milo, and I step out. The two of them flank me as we approach the entrance. I place my hand on the door handle, the heavy metal groans as I pull it toward us. *Oh good, announcing our arrival.* I can't help the amusement as my men follow me inside. Matt is the one who greets us this time.

"Mr. Ludovico? What are you –" His question is cut off when I raise my hand indicating I don't want to talk here.

"How about we head into the office, Matt." My suggestion is a command, and we all know it. Matt's expression is filled with annoyance as he leads us down the same hallway he did the last time we were here. Before we step into the office, Milo speaks low in Michael's ear and leaves us before the door is shut, leaving it two against one. I remain as neutral as possible while I wait for Matt to speak.

I pull the loaded Glock from my holster vest and take a seat at the large leather chair behind his desk. After laying my right leg over my left, I rest the gun on my thigh, stroking the metal like a pet. Matt's body goes rigid, which only fuels my delight.

"To what do I owe the pleasure, Mr. Ludovico?" His tone is clipped, which only makes his fear transparent.

"What do you know about Bastian Caprioni?" I cut straight to it. There's no reason to hide why I'm here. Matt's face turns into a mask of stark terror. I don't miss the way he stumbles backward at the mention of that name. He tries to steady himself, but the damage is done. "You may want to just give me the information you have now, otherwise it will just make everything a hell of a lot more painful for you." The faux friendship in my voice is quite comical, but it calms him enough to open up.

"All I know is that Mateo had plans for Nina that you ruined by claiming her the way you did. He's been a maniac about losing his golden ticket." There's a tremble in Matt's voice which makes his confession all the more fucked. "Bastian was expected to have the girl back at Mateo's home at some point between last night and this morning."

The office door opens and Milo steps in. He takes his place next to Michael and nods a quick confirmation.

"Well, Matt. This has been fun, but I'm going to need you to sit here for a few moments while I decide what to do with you." Without another word, I stand and carefully place my Glock back where it belongs. Milo and Michael follow closely behind. There is no sound coming from Matt's office, which is a bonus for us.

When we reach the exit, Milo rigs the door so it can't be opened from either direction. The two of them fall into step behind me as we head for the car. This time, I slide into the passenger seat and pull my phone out of my jacket pocket again. After a few taps on the screen, I open the camera and start recording —the building and button in my hand are both in the frame.

"Boss," I hear Milo's voice as a small black device is held out in front of me. I grin as I place it in my palm.

I hold the device with the large button face up and gently glide my thumb over the temptation before finally pressing down. A chorus of explosions sound as the bombs Milo placed around the building blow. We begin to drive off in the opposite direction, and I press the button to end the recording.

I pull up a blank message in our encrypted messaging app.

Come after what's mine again, I dare you. You will beg me to kill you after what I have planned. [Video Attached]

I step into the house and am hit with the intoxicating scent of Mrs. D's spicy sausage Bolognese. Fuck me, it's been years. As I meander toward the kitchen, I hear the voices of Mrs. D, my mother, and Nina; the latter of whom is laughing, and my heart warms at the sound. When I step through the threshold into the kitchen, I see Nina and Mrs. D cooking together. The sight of her coming out of her shell and doing something she's never had the opportunity to do before instantly has my dick swelling in my pants. *Down boy.* Thankfully my mother takes that moment to pull me aside, which instantly ices the growing arousal.

"How did he get into the house? I heard something about the cameras, but Milo swore the men to secrecy, which I don't fucking appreciate, by the way." She rapidly spews out her frustration from last night – which, fair.

After I explain to her what I know she breathes a small sigh of relief, but her eyes lock in on me.

"Giovanni, *mio vita*. I know you had no intention of returning to this life or the life I had planned for you." She shakes her head like she's trying to forget the past decade and a half. "But now that you're here and you've taken your position as Capo, you need to make sure everyone knows you're not to be fucked with."

Chapter 18

Nina

My footsteps echo through the large foyer as I cross the open space, headed back toward the kitchen. My steps begin to falter as the two women who have taken me under their wing come into view. Vanna is seated at the kitchen island laughing at something Jade said while she's cooking. Instead of joining in on the conversation, I take a seat next to Vanna. My mind still whirls from the events of this morning.

What does it say about me, that seeing the man I fell asleep with last night kill a man isn't the part that has me flustered?

I'm not sure how long I've been sitting here before I feel a cold gentle hand clasp over mine. I look up to see a worried Jade. There was a time when the idea of being touched like this, even this little gesture, would have been a foreign concept. Now, after only a week, my eyes well with tears at the kindness from this woman.

"Nina, would you like something for breakfast?" She squeezes gently, her lips tilt down into a frown.

I wipe the unshed tears from my eyes and force as bright a smile as I can while offering a reassuring nod.

"Thank you. A cinnamon bun and a hot tea would be wonderful." My request is met with a raised brow. My pulse begins to race as I take in her inquisitive glance. "What?"

Jade and Vanna's eyes meet. A silent conversation passes between them.

"Hot tea? You haven't had tea since you've been here. What gives, Sweetheart?" Vanna asks the question that they apparently both want to know.

I lift and drop my shoulder in a half shrug, unsure of how to explain what is going through my mind. A few moments later, my breakfast is placed before me. The two women who have been a source of comfort during this transition continue their conversation as if I'm not here. My heart rate slows as they ignore me. I'm not sure if it's the healthiest way to cope, but after being alone for so long, I need to internally process before I can verbalize my thoughts.

My mouth waters as I take my first bite, the mixture of the sweet cream cheese icing and spicy cinnamon explode on my tongue. With my eyes closed, I allow myself to get lost in the medley of flavors. Jade added something a little different to it this time. My eyes fly open, and I find her staring at me like she's been waiting for me to figure it out.

"What did you do?" I ask as I take another bite, not waiting for a response. Jade grins at me as I lift the steaming mug of tea to my lips and take a cautious sip.

"If you can tell I changed something so small as adding a dash of cardamom from one bite, you're cooking dinner with me tonight, kid." Jade chuckles and turns away, disappearing from the room for another task.

My eyes drop back down to my now empty plate. I hop down from the chair and take my dishes to the sink. When I turn around, Vanna is staring at me.

"Would you mind taking a walk with me?" My question comes out as a whisper, but her lips pull into a knowing grin.

"Of course, Dear, let's go." She steps down and sidles up next to me as we walk side by side to the back door. I can sense Abel and Rand behind us now without the need to glance back.

I stop at one of the large rose bushes and lean in, taking a deep breath of the beautiful floral scent. My eyes prick with confusion and joy. *It's the strangest combination of emotions. Zero out of ten, don't recommend.* I turn toward Vanna instead of continuing through the greenery, ready to rip off the proverbial band aid.

"What is it, Honey?" Vanna's maternal nature peaks through as she pulls me into a tight embrace.

I bury my face in my hands as I gather the words and confidence to share my reason for dragging her out here.

"I don't know what's going on with – well anything, really." Once I begin, the words start to tumble out, the thoughts continue much easier. "When I'm with Giovanni I feel more comfortable and at home than I've ever felt. Last night, you know what happened..." I pause waiting for acknowledgement which she provides in a small jerk of her head. "He forced me to stay in his room last night. I've never – I mean, obviously I've never – but I've never shared a room overnight with a man, let alone a bed. But I woke up and I was basically wrapped around him like a Koala on a eucalyptus tree."

At some point during my confession, we must have begun walking again because I realize we're approaching the gorgeous wrought-iron bench set under one of the smaller trees. She waves her hand in front of me to take a seat, our shoulders are touching as I continue to spew the word vomit at her.

"I just – I don't understand why I feel the way I do. When he walks in the room my tummy does weird things that makes my heart stutter in my chest at the same time." When I glance over at Vanna she's trying and failing to hide her smile. "What? What is it?"

She shakes her head and holds a hand up in surrender. "Sweetheart, you spent a lot of time reading and watching movies when you were – well, before you came here, right?"

I nod, unsure where she's going with this. My eyes stay locked on her as she covers her mouth trying to hide her amusement. I let out a groan and begin to stand, but she pulls me back down, her dark eyes sparkle with delight as she takes me in.

"Remember in those stories, whether it was on page or on screen, there would be couples that end up together usually sharing a kiss at the very end?" Her voice is so soft, as she tries to hold back laughter. I jerk my head in an annoyed nod. Her shoulders begin to steady as the amusement subsides and cups my face between her delicate hands. "Sweetheart, you are falling for my Giovanni."

The headboard of Giovanni's bed is cool on my back as I lean against it. My mind is a maze of chaos and confusion as I run through the conversation with Vanna in my mind again. Who am I kidding? It's been playing on repeat since I made my way back into the solace of our room. *Our* room. I don't even know what any of this means.

I allow myself to think back to the books I've read and movies I've watched with Cece. Jane and Stan's sweet first crush in the old book with hearts all over the cover that I've read so many times the title, Fifteen, is worn off. Most recently, she had a book peeking out of her bag that I may have borrowed for the night when she wasn't looking. It was a fun book about a female millionaire, which was different. I liked it. *I wonder if I can get any more of that author's books now.* My insides were gooey after reading that.

A Walk to Remember was a beautiful story and the first time Landon and Jamie kissed I felt like my heart would explode. The tension between the two was intoxicating, I've wanted that since Cece allowed me to watch that movie. I mean, without the cancer, obviously.

Huh...

My lips part with a sharp gasp. Pinhead chooses that moment to climb into my lap. His tail slaps violently against me. He stands on his hind legs stretching up to my face where he butts his furry face against my chin and wraps his paws around my neck in a hug. I fold my arms around him and hold him against my chest. Tears begin to fall down my cheeks, and I take in a shaky breath.

There is no doubt in my mind that I am falling for Giovanni, and that scares the hell out of me. When I came here, my only thought was freedom. Freedom to find myself, to become the woman I'm meant to be. But what if the woman I'm supposed to be is the one at his side, helping him in his role as Capo?

A sudden knock on the bedroom door pulls me out of my thoughts. My head jerks up to see Jade standing there with her arms crossed and a wide, knowing smile on her face. The corners of her eyes crinkle with her grin as she takes me in.

"Are you ready to help me make dinner, Dear?" Jade's gentle voice masks her joy, but it's clear as day in her eyes. At least for me.

I chuckle and shake my head before I pull Pinhead off of my neck. He chirps in response as if to express his displeasure. When I hop off the bed and begin to cross the room, she starts back to the kitchen. I pad through the hallway, taking in the surroundings a little differently. Could I be his partner in this house? In this life? Does he even want that?

Shit, I'm getting ahead of myself. I don't even know how to broach the subject with him.

Tears prick at the corners of my eyes when I think about telling Giovanni. What if he doesn't feel the same way? I don't know that I could handle losing Jade or Vanna. Not to mention Abe. He's become such a good friend. I wipe the moisture from my cheeks as my feet hit the tile floor of the kitchen to find Jade coating the kitchen counter with a dusting of flour. I must look as confused as I feel because Jade's eyes lock on me and she chuckles.

"Come on over here, sweet girl, I made pasta dough from scratch." Her smile lights up the room which only seems to calm my nerves.

Placing one foot in front of the other, I cautiously approach the counter like it's a bomb that's about to go off. I'm not sure why, but this seems like more of a daunting task than I initially expected. When I reach the counter and peek down at the lump of pasta dough Jade begins to laugh. Her entire body vibrates with laughter as she takes me in. My skin heats with embarrassment.

Thirty minutes later we're done cutting the noodles into shape while Jade and Vanna have been sharing stories of Giovanni growing up, which has been heartwarming to say the least.

"I remember the first time you attempted to show him around the kitchen," Vanna teases Jade who snorts in response.

Her smile widens into a grin as the memory unfolds behind her eyes.

"Oh, you mean the time he started a fire?" Her shoulders shake with laughter as she continues. "Picture it, a six-year-old little boy with dark waves mussed after a wrestling match with my Anthony." Jade pauses when she mentions her late husband, I instinctively reach out to take her hand. Her fingers wrap around mine as she squeezes reassuringly. "The boy had been begging me to teach him to cook for weeks. Finally, Frederico had enough and gave me his blessing to share my knowledge with the kid. I left him at the counter on a step stool to roll out the dough much like I've done with you, yet he decided when my back was turned to grab a missing ingredient from the fridge that he needed to play with the stove." Jade doesn't miss a beat and seems to revel in sharing his history with me.

My chest tightens at the imagery she paints of a young Giovanni trying to help, only to cause chaos. A smooth voice breaks through the conversation and my body stiffens.

"If I remember correctly, you are the one who left a dish towel on the range." Giovanni chuckles darkly as he enters the room.

My gaze lifts to find him but before I can utter a greeting, Vanna stands and rushes to him. She whispers something to him and they disappear out the side door.

Jade chooses that moment to pull my attention back to her. She talks me through plating our food and guides me to the table to set our places. I hear the door open when I set Vanna and Jade's plates in place.

He crosses the space in a fluid motion, his broad shoulders fill out his dark suit so beautifully. A crease forms between his brows as his warm chocolate gaze roams over me. I can feel him catalog every part of me that he can see, and before I know it his thumb and forefinger have my chin tilted so I'm staring up at him. Our eyes lock on one another as we gaze into each other's souls.

"Hey, Short Stack." Giovanni's eyes sparkle when he uses the nickname. "How was your day, *Bella*?"

"Hi," the response comes out in a whispered breath. My cheeks heat under his gaze. "It was good." My heart stutters in my chest when he swipes this thumb against my lower lip, our eyes never tearing away from one another. After a span of I'm not sure how long and he's satisfied with whatever he sees, he takes a step back allowing me space to breathe and regain my ability to function.

Giovanni's hand lands on the small of my back over the thin fabric of my shirt, the heat that radiates from his skin sends a jolt of electricity through my body at the simple contact. He guides me to the table, pulling out a chair for me, the one I had intended for Vanna on his right. When my glance lands on her, she jerks her head in a subtle nod.

I slide down into the seat which he pushes in gently behind me. Vanna and Jade take their seats on the other side of the table, the two of them so obviously tickled by our interaction. I want to throw my napkin at them. *Is that normal?* The four of us sit in silence for a few minutes while we eat. The sweet and spicy flavors mix together so perfectly in the sausage Bolognese that I let out a happy sigh.

"Fuck," Giovanni groans, startling me. The two women across from me snort simultaneously. They actually snort. His brow furrows, his gaze turning into a glare. That is, until he looks back at me and his face softens.

I force myself to stare at my plate while I push around the food, suddenly too nervous to eat. Jade and Vanna are speaking softly to one another while we sit there finishing our meal, or while they finish their meal. I bring a fork full to my lips, knowing that if I don't force myself to eat a little more, I'll hate myself when I lay down for the night and can only think about food. I lift a shoulder in a shrug as I remember it happening so many times before, when I had no control over my food.

"Mother, why didn't she get the gift I left for her?" Giovanni's voice cuts through the noise in my head.

I jerk my head up. My gaze darts between the two of them, trying to understand what he's talking about. Vanna's shoulders lift and fall in a dramatic shrug.

"We had more important things to worry about. Girl talk, and all." She winks at me as a smirk dances across her lips. "Then she and Jade decided to make dinner, so you see darling, there was no time."

Giovanni's fingers are entwined with mine as he leads me through the house to his office. When we step inside, he stands at the door silently waiting for me to give him permission to close it, which he seems to do every time he wants privacy with me. My heart explodes in my chest when I realize what he's been doing. I smile as I nod my permission and take a seat on the same couch as the first night I was here. A soft click sounds when the door latches closed. He crosses the room to his desk to pick something up before he joins me. His knee presses against my thigh as I wait with bated breath for him to explain what's going on. He hands over a box that looks small inside of his large palm. It takes a moment for my brain to register what I'm looking at. I lift the top off to see a sleek, shiny new cell phone.

"Giova – I – you. I've never – thank you." My eyes well with tears that begin to fall freely. "Why are you so good to me?"

The question is out before I can stop myself. He chuckles as he pulls the phone out of the box and presses the button onto the side which brings the screen to life; it shines so brightly as it cycles through the different images as it boots up.

"*Bella*, you are the strongest woman I've ever met. Every single day you have been fighting to survive without realizing it." He cups my cheek in his palm and I lean into the warmth, "I want to take care of you while allowing you to be who you are meant to be. You need the freedom to find out who that woman is, but I also want to make sure you can always reach me."

As soon as he finishes his explanation, the phone dings in his hand. He smirks as he hands over the device. I glance down at the screen to see his name, when I tap the screen, a message appears.

Johnny

N ina's brow furrows as she reads the text I sent earlier this morning. When her gaze turns back to me her mouth parts slowly and closes again. With how well she's been handling the number of people in and out of the house, it's hard to believe she's never gone out in general, let alone gone shopping.

Her voice is light and full of hope as she asks the question, "Go where?"

My lips turn up at the corner with a devilish smirk. I pull her a little closer and her leg ends up draped over my knee when I reply.

"I know a boutique that my mother likes. I can get in touch with the owner and have them close it down so it's just us and a salesperson." My hand lays gently on her knee, knowing I'm pushing my damn luck, but fuck, the need to be close to her is becoming overwhelming. "*Bella*, you've never had that experience. You may not be ready to face the Black Friday crowds yet, but I think you deserve the joy of being able to pick out your own clothing."

My brain functions in slow motion as I watch Nina launch herself onto my lap. Her perfectly tight ass rests on my thigh as she wraps her arms around my neck. I freeze for a moment, unsure what to do, or what is too much for her. That is until soft sobs have her shoulders shaking as she buries her face into my neck. I wrap my arms around her tiny frame. My body cocoons her from the outside world, at least for a few minutes. When she gathers herself, she props herself up, pushing slightly away from my chest so she can look at me. Her palms press firmly against my chest as she stares into my eyes, her shining light grey eyes bore themselves into my soul.

"Thank you, Giovanni." The words come out in a gentle breath, "I can't tell you what this means to me. You are the kindest man." She sucks in a breath as my thumb caresses her spine. Her cheeks flush at the small touch. I do my best to stifle the smile that tries to form on my lips.

Nina breaks our gaze a minute later as she stands, stepping back allowing me room to get up myself. I pull my phone out from my suit's jacket pocket and tap on the screen to pull up my message thread with Michael.

Giovanni:

Have Tabatha clear out Threads with the exception of one salesperson. We'll be leaving in about twenty minutes.

A message bounces back less than a minute later.

Michael:

Done, she said Janelle will be there waiting on you.

I can't help but grin as I lead Nina back into our room so she can grab a pair of shoes. She only has one pair of sneakers that look worn out. I make a mental note to make sure a replacement pair is delivered by the end of the evening since she likes more strenuous exercises. I don't think the fashion forward tennis shoes they'll have at Threads will work for her.

A little over a half an hour later, we're pulling into the parking lot outside of the small boutique my mother swears by. The exterior of the building looks to be freshly painted a pale-yellow. I push open my door and step out, closing it quickly behind me before I rush around to the passenger side. My grip on the handle slips as soon as I see the awe in her expression. I can't stop the grin from forming on my face as I pull open her door.

Once she is at my side, I loop her arm with mine. She grips my wrist as she begins to tremble. I place my other hand over top of hers and smile down at her before pressing my lips against her hair.

"It's going to be ok, *Bella.* I've got a guarantee only one other person will be in the building with us." I whisper and grin against her ear when I feel the goosebumps cover her skin. With that, she melts into me a little and allows me to lead her around the building.

The front door is a large glass panel, which looks like it was recently wiped down. I tap my knuckles against the door and a woman who looks to be in her mid-forties approaches. Her platinum blonde hair is pulled back into a tight sleek bun. She's slender and a bit taller than Nina. However, unlike my girl, this woman looks like she has no personality. The door swings open and the woman gestures for us to join her.

"Good evening, I'm Janelle." Her previously annoyed expression morphs into one of false warmth. *Yeah, I don't like this bitch already.* "It's so nice to have you here this evening, Mr. Ludovico. What is it that you're looking for tonight?"

I eye her warily, but knowing Nina is already anxious over this outing, I wave it off as over protectiveness.

"Hi Janelle, this is Nina." I grin at the woman on my arm before returning my gaze to Janelle. "She is in need of a new wardrobe. Anything she wants, absolutely no limits." I feel a gentle squeeze on my hand and notice Nina staring up at me with a wander in her eyes.

We follow Janelle toward the back of the shop to a maze of clothing racks which appears to have an array of shirts in different styles hanging on them. Nina freezes when she sees the options, but I urge her forward.

"It's alright, Short Stack, do your worst." I wink down at her and step away just enough that she can find her footing on her own even if I'm only an arm's length away. Her body goes rigid momentarily when I'm no longer touching her, but when she realizes I've not gone anywhere, she relaxes a bit. After a few cautious steps toward the clothing my heart warms when she reaches out to get a better look at a few items.

Her chest lifts and falls steadily as she breathes without the anxiety she was experiencing when we first got here. My lips turn upward into a wide grin as I watch her. A few moments into her search through the clothing racks, I see the wall of shoes which reminds me of what I asked to have at the house before we get home. I excuse myself, promising I'll only be right outside.

I step just outside the door and press the call icon on Michael's contact. A rush of cool evening air sends a chill through me as I lift the device to my ear. The line rings only once before he picks up. An annoyed grunt sounds as he answers the call.

"Get out of whoever you're fucking for two seconds." I bark at him, unable to hide my amusement; it ends on a choked laugh. "I need you to have something taken care of for me before we get back."

A muffled curse comes through the phone followed by a soft whimper. My lips twitch into a crooked grin. After some more rustling he comes back onto the line.

"The fuck do you want?" Michael's grumble only amuses me more. "Aren't you supposed to be out with your woman that you refuse to claim?"

I snarl at the mention of Nina. "Shut it. I need you to have a new pair of sneakers delivered to the house in the next hour. The ones she has are falling apart."

Michael chokes out a laugh, "Are you fucking kidding me? Why couldn't you call Abel for this shit?"

I lean against the doorframe staring into the street as I respond. "As much as I appreciate Abel, he's not quite as efficient as you are. Get it done." I grin as I press the button to disconnect the call. With a quick glance at my watch, I realize I've been outside for ten minutes. I pull the door open toward me and step back inside.

Soft sobs are what greet me as I cross the large retail space filled with racks of clothes on either side of me. My heart crumbles into a million pieces when I reach the back where I left Nina. She's cowering with her back against a wall tucked between a bench and a mannequin and curled into herself. Her knees are pulled tight into her chest like she's protecting herself from something. I rush to her side; my palms cup her cheeks and try to lift her to look at me.

"*Bella*, Short Stack. I'm right here. What happened?" My words come out so quickly I can barely understand myself.

Nina's inconsolable, she's disassociated so badly I don't know that she even registers me here. Rage, anger, and fury heat my blood to the verge of boiling when I turn to find Janelle standing on the other side of the room with a wicked smirk on her face. A vicious snarl passes my lips as I approach, my body crowding her space. I stand tall knowing my massive frame is intimidating as fuck to anyone, but especially a woman. Usually, I'd be respectful of a woman's space, but not this time.

"What the fuck did you do?" I growl at Janelle. My hands ball into fists at my side as I watch her stupid fucking face fight a smile. When she shrugs as if it's no big deal, I lose what little composure I have left and move quickly. My hand wraps tightly around her throat as I slowly begin to back her up. "You're going to tell me what the fuck you did or said to her, understand?"

Janelle rolls her eyes like she's not in any danger. *Oh, please bitch, give me a fucking reason.* "I didn't tell her anything untrue." She scoffs with her response.

I can feel my lip curl like a goddamn wolf as another growl rumbles free. My grip tightens around her throat as the anger continues to surge through me, and I lift her just enough so that her toes are the only thing touching the ground. Her nails dig into my wrist and hand as I keep her in place.

"Care to share with the class, cunt? Because when I walked out that door, she may have been anxious, but she had a smile on her face." My chest heaves as I snarl and spew obscenities at her.

Janelle's eyes go wide as she takes me in. Less than a minute later she's whimpering against my still tight grip. I release her just enough so she's able to speak.

"I told her that she was a gold digger and no man in your position of power would want her. She should just go back to her daddy." Tears begin to fall down her flushed cheeks when I tighten my hold once again. Janelle's nails begin to dig into the thin skin on my hand again, tearing it open as she tries to find purchase in my flesh. The rest of her admission comes out in pathetic gasps. "She doesn't belong with you."

I cock a brow at her, there is no way she could really be such a cunt. I know by the way her throat is responding to my grip, she'll have bruises in the morning. I can't bring myself to give a fuck.

"You know, I've made it a point in my time on this earth," I begin. "–to not bring pain to or kill women. However, right now in this moment, you're lucky you're not chopped in pieces on this fucking floor." I push her hard against the wall, an audible thud sounds when the back of her head bounces off the plaster. "Get the fuck out of here."

My breath hitches when I turn back toward where Nina is still cowered, exactly where I left her. She looks so small and defeated; it only serves to piss me off even more. I cross the space to her and kneel in front of her.

"Short Stack, can you hear me?" I try. "Come on, Sweetheart. I need you to look at me." When no response or reaction comes, I slide my arms under her small body and lift her into my arms. After I nearly stumble when I go to stand to my normal height, I straighten myself and hold her as close to my chest as I can. Nina manages to bury her face into the crook of my neck as I carry her to the car.

Nina's entire body shakes as sobs tear through her. Every muscle in her body is vibrating with anxiety, sadness, and anger. I've had her in our bed for the last hour with no change of behavior or ability to respond to me. My arms wrap around her as I attempt to hold her tight and offer some comfort, yet I can't pull her out of her own mind.

As I roll my stiff neck, trying to bring some blood flow back to the muscles, a box catches my eye that wasn't there before we had left. I stand and pad over to the recent addition to our room. I kneel and flip the lid open to find the shoes I had asked Michael to get for her. With a smile tugging at my lips, I pull out my phone, sending a quick message with another request. I stand back to my full height and carry the shoes with me.

Nina is still curled into herself laying on the bed. I move back to her side and lift her into my arms without a word. The shoes are still in my hand as I carry her through the house and walk us to the gym she has spent so much time in. As soon as I enter the space, I carefully place her on a weight bench and remove one shoe at a time. I toss them out of the way before I slide the new sneakers on and tighten the laces. These will have better stability for what I'm about to try. Once I'm done, I rise onto my knees and take her face between my hands. My eyes bore into her soul as I speak.

"*Bella*, everything she said was a lie and deep down, you know that." I say gently as I pull her into a standing position and guide her to where I want her. My back hits something and it pushes me back toward her, but I keep my footing. "I want you to see her face and let the cunt have it. You hear me? Show her you're not to be fucked with."

I step out of the way, dropping my hands to my side as I watch Nina. She finally glances at me; she's got some life back to her. Nina half-heartedly swings against the punching bag, and I can't help but let out a snort. She becomes irritated after that, but doesn't direct her irritation at me. She focuses on the bag. After the third swing, she really gets into what she's doing. She spins, landing a roundhouse kick on the bag, and it swings away from her farther than it had before. She squeals as she jumps in celebration, but she steps too close into the return path and the bag hits her square in the stomach and she lands a few feet away on her ass.

"Fuck!" I curse under my breath as I rush over to steady the bag before scrambling to get to Nina. I kneel next to her and take in the vision before me. Her eyes go wide for a moment before she's laughing so hard she can't catch her breath. It's a wonderful sound that I could get lost in. She has a dimple on the left side of her mouth that she's never smiled big enough for me to see before. Her amusement is contagious at this moment, and I can't help laughing with her.

Before I can ask if she's ok, she lunges forward. Her arms fold tight around my neck as she sits on my lap, her legs draped over mine. Her face is buried in the crook of my neck again, but this time, it's not in sadness, it's with a sense of peace.

"Thank you, Giovanni." She whispers against my neck, sending goose bumps dancing across my skin.

I cup the back of her head; her beautiful strawberry locks feel like silk under my touch.

"Nina, I would do anything for you, even if that means spilling blood."

Chapter 20

Nina

Giovanni's warmth feels so good against my body. My mind is still whirling with chaos after what happened tonight. I press my palms against his chest to separate myself from the comfort that he brings, still too anxious to allow myself to go there until I know how he feels. The moment my face is in front of his, Giovanni's smooth hands cup my cheeks. His thumb swipes against my lips which makes me melt right back into him.

"Nina" My name is a whispered plea on his lips.

Our eyes stay locked on one another. I feel my chest and face become heated under his delicious brown gaze. My lips part in a soft gasp when one hand moves to the back of my neck, keeping me in place.

"Gio–" I begin, but I'm cut off when his soft lips press firmly against mine. The kiss is gentle, but so full of passion and heat. I can feel his hesitation when I go still, unsure what to do with my body. My legs are still draped over his. I lift my hands to grab handfuls of his hair as I rearrange myself. My knees rest on either side of his hips as I lower myself back into his lap. A guttural groan leaves him as he urges my lips apart with his tongue. I whimper when his tongue enters my mouth. Our kiss, which began as a sweet, soft moment, has escalated. I can feel him hardening under me. I like what I feel, but have no clue what to do with it. Giovanni's tongue explores every part of my mouth as he savors my taste.

A slew of soft whimpers and moans roll past my lips. I can't get enough of him. His hands grip my hips so hard I'll have bruises in the morning. I can't find a reason to care. Especially when he pushes me down and guides me back and forth, grinding against the rock in his trousers, which only makes the heat in my belly become molten. He pulls away gently with a growl reverberating deep in his chest. Giovanni presses a few more quick pecks against my lips as he takes me in. I can't help but stare into those beautiful brown eyes once again as he presses his forehead against mine. Both of us are panting, trying to catch our breath. *"Sei mio, Bella"* his declaration makes my heart beat at a thunderous rhythm in my chest.

"Sì, tuo" I reply coyly, thankful that I'm a quick study. Though, I doubt I could say much more than that right now.

His bright brown eyes go wide when my response is in the same Italian tongue he used on me. My shoulders become lighter as my body shakes with laughter. When the laughter finally subsides and I smile widely at him, I notice him swallow hard but don't think to ask about it.

"Jade and your mom have been teaching me during the day."

Giovanni's expression changes to something warm as he leans in and presses another quick kiss to my lips before we both stand to our feet. I notice him adjusting himself and can't help but flush, knowing I caused that reaction.

"Are you doing ok?" His playfulness has vanished with the question.

I let out a long breath before I reply. "I've done kickboxing with what few videos Cece allowed or was allowed to provide me. I'm still not sure how that worked." My shoulders lift and fall in a shrug. "I was able to mimic what I saw there, but it wasn't one of my favorite workouts because the bag can only teach you so much. I want to learn for real one day," I smile wistfully.

I can feel his eyes on me as I begin to step away when he rushes up beside me, pulling me flush against his chest again.

"I'll have one of the guys teach you." His grin turns into a grimace after a moment and he shakes his head, "Never mind. I've seen what you wear in here. I'll teach you."

I stop, pressing my hands against his hard pecs ready to shove him away. "What do you mean?"

Giovanni's eyes nearly roll into the back of his head. "*Bella*, you hold more beauty and charm in your little finger than most women do in their entire body." He levels me with just one glance that somehow makes my insides scorch while feeling giddy at the same time. What is this? "I've seen the way my men look at you when you're fully clothed. There's no fucking way I'm letting my men around you close enough to spar when you're in a sports bra and yoga pants. Absolutely fucking not, Short Stack." For the first time, the pet name sounds like a warning, and it only makes me hotter.

I press my lips together in a tight line trying to fight back my amusement, but a snort sneaks out as I eye him. "Abel has been nothing but a gentleman since he's been my shadow. He didn't even want to help me put on sunblock because he didn't feel comfortable touching me."

A low growl emanates from deep in his throat, his eyes darken as he grips my chin and brings my lips to his, but he doesn't kiss me. At least not right away. "Fine, but if he touches you, he's dead." He declares as he crushes his mouth to mine. I giggle into the exchange as his arms wrap around my waist.

We begin to make our way out of the gym and back upstairs. Giovanni slows his pace to match mine.

"I was asking about what happened tonight at Threads." His tone is unreadable. He sucks in a breath before expanding, "That's not how I wanted tonight to go. I'm so fucking sorry it happened, but it never will again. She'll be lucky if I allow her to continue living in this town"

I stop abruptly and spin on my heel to face him. "Wait, what?"

The corners of his lips dance with the most delicious and mis-chievous smirk that the space between my legs begins to throb. What the hell is happening to me? His hand grasps my wrist but not hard enough to hurt, just to pull along with him. I nearly trip over myself when Giovanni comes to a stop when we reach his office. His spine straightens, and he stands at his full height as we step inside. I peek around his huge statuesque frame to see Michael standing next to a pretty blonde woman who appears to be around the same age as Vanna. I'm sure the question is clear on my face when I meet Michael's gaze but he doesn't respond. Instead, Giovanni turns back toward me and casually guides me to the chair behind his desk.

"What is going on Giovanni? Why am I here?" The woman is obviously angry, but I have no clue who she is or why she would be upset with him. I dig my nails into the arm rests when she yells at him, I don't like him being spoken to like this.

"I brought you here as a courtesy to my mother instead of just having you killed, Auntie Tabs. And it's Johnny." Giovanni's hard mask is in place as he speaks to her, and pulls a gun from his back slamming it on the desk next to him. "After all, it would upset my *Madre* should I have your throat slit without at least hearing you out."

My jaw drops as my eyes dart back and forth between the two of them.

"What happened?" Her throat bobs as she swallows hard, obviously scared.

Giovanni leans in front of the desk. The back of his thighs presses against the oversized ornate furniture partially obscuring my view. His thick, muscular arms cross over his chest as he glares at her. I can see her jerk her head to look at Michael before returning to Giovanni.

He lets her bathe in silence for several moments before he begins to explain what happened; what Janelle had said to me, how I was treated, and my reaction. I flinch when he explains his perspective. I'm more infuriated that I upset him. After all, he's the reason I'm free. I want to make his life easier, not harder.

When he's finally done reiterating the events of the evening, the woman he's referred to as his aunt jumps to her feet. Her expression shows just how appalled she is. She takes a step toward me, and my body goes stiff. I see Michael grip her right bicep to keep her in place. He and Giovanni have a silent exchange before he releases her, but Michael's hand is steady on the gun in his holster, ready for anything.

The woman drops to her knees in front of me and clasps my hands in hers as tears stream down her perfectly made-up face. Dark streaks form under her eyes from her mascara as she speaks.

"I am so sorry, Nina. I would have never hired her had I known she was like this." She gasps for air as she continues, her shoulders begin to shake as she continues to sob at my feet. "That is not the company I keep and my goal has and always will be to remain as inclusive as possible. I don't stand for bullying. I swear to you, I will handle this immediately."

My heart beats frantically in my chest as I listen to her words.

"If you'd be open to it, I would be happy to personally bring all of my inventory here so you can have a better experience in the comfort of your own home." I can see the plea in her offer.

We've been in Giovanni's office for upwards of an hour and I just want to get out of here. My gaze bores into Tabs' dark blue eyes and nod.

"I would like that, thank you." I pause, keeping my stare trained on her, "But if I'm treated that way again, I will not be breaking down. I will make anything that he would do look like child's play." I nod my head in Giovanni's direction, who has an amused grin spread wide across his face.

The clicks and clacks of high heels against the hardwood floor sound from the hallway as the owner comes closer. Tabs' eyes are so wide you could probably pluck them out of her skull so easily. *Wait, where the fuck did that come from?*

"Hey! What are you doing here, Tabatha?" Vanna calls, her voice full of so much excitement, if I hadn't just witnessed what happened in here it would be infectious. Vanna turns to Giovanni, whose face is a mask of calm.

"She can discuss that with you while you show her out." He jerks his head for Tabatha to leave. He turns to Michael as soon as they're gone and barks at him to leave before he faces me once again.

My gaze is trained on the firecracker in front of me. Jesus Christ, I didn't think she'd have that in her *yet*. This woman has been underestimated her entire life. She is going to leave a trail of bodies in her wake, and she doesn't even realize it. I close the distance between the two of us and drag her into my arms. She lets out a breathy gasp when I crush her against my chest.

"I have no idea where the fuck that fierceness came from, *Bella*. But fuck me, that was sexy as hell." Her eyes are bright with pride as I continue, "You are so fucking incredible and you don't even realize it." I admit before crashing my lips against hers. She parts for me, allowing my tongue access to her own eager mouth. A soft whimper passes from her into me as I explore every part I can. Our tongues come together in a salacious dance that has my cock stiffening in my pants. The pressure of her body pressed against mine has me ready to explode right here.

Nina stiffens and presses her delicate hands against my chest as she pulls away from the kiss. Her face is that gorgeous shade of pink I love so much as she glances down at the monster not very well hidden between my legs. It must have scared the hell out of her.

"Shit. I'm sorry, *Bella*." I internally scold myself; I need to work on my control. I lean down and press a soft kiss against her forehead before tearing myself away and snatching my Glock from the desk. "I'll be back in a bit; I'm going to go take care of some things."

As soon as my back is to her, I squeeze my dick as I adjust myself, trying to relieve some of the pressure. My feet move swiftly with purpose as I weave my way through my home to get to the basement.

I shove my gun into the waistband of my trousers to free my hands so that I can pull my phone from my pocket. I tap the screen a few times and send quick messages to Milo and Michael instructing them to meet me at the cell.

I pull open the heavy door and descend the stairs to find the cell where my grandfather's body was left not too long ago, now occupied by the motherfucker who nearly allowed Nina to be taken from me. When I find Danny Boy standing guard at the entrance, I nod at him to take his leave.

My eyes take in the man who is cowering on the cot in the corner of the room. My face turns into a scowl as I observe the asshole. I feel Michael and Milo's presence before they even have a chance to speak. My hand lands on the latch of the cell door and I pull the heavy metal toward me, allowing access to Rich. His eyes dart up to find mine, his skin ghostly pale. My lips turn up into a wicked grin as I shove my hand into my pocket to find the knife that is never too far away.

"We're going to have a," I pause as I take a step closer. "Friendly," my sinister inflection at the end of the word has him pressing further into the wall. "Conversation, Rich."

The man lets out constant, shrill, pained whimpers that have me ready to strangle him. I haven't even touched the motherfucker yet. I pull the knife from inside my pocket and release the blade. The glint of the metal flashes in his eyes before I toss it into the air and catch the knife by the handle waving it in front of Rich to taunt him.

"I'm sorry, Johnny. I didn't mean to –" He sobs as I pull him from his position on the cot by his throat and drag him to the center of the room. I feel his throat bob as he swallows hard under my grip. Loud scrapes of metal against concrete sound as one of my men brings in a chair to strap Rich to. Milo and Michael quickly work together as I lower the man into the seat, restraining him before I release my grip.

Instead of speaking, I wind my arm back, with my hand bawled into a fist, and swing hard. The punch lands with an audible crack when my fist collides with his eye. I grin when I feel the eye socket crunch under my fist from the impact. Rich howls out in pain as blood trickles down the side of his face.

"So, you thought that a nap while you were stationed to guard Nina was a smart fucking move?" I snarl as I force his head up to meet my gaze with my blade pressed firmly under his chin. "How long have you been working for Barone?"

Rich shakes his head and spits out a mouthful of saliva and blood. His lips part as he tries to speak, but I'm too worked up to allow him to even attempt to give a chance to explain himself. I quickly swipe my knife against the dirty shirt he's wearing to shred the material. When his bare chest is on display, I slice through the skin just enough to draw blood. He hisses at the sting of the blade and curses as he forces himself to look back up at me.

"Johnny, I swear. I would never!" His sobs only serve to fuel my anger and I dig my knife into him, slicing along the ridge of every muscle his fitness routine has blessed him with. Rich's screams become frantic with every drop of blood I spill. "No! I have the flu!" His whales stop me in my tracks.

I look back at Milo and Michael who look as stunned as I feel. Rich groans as he pleads with me to hear him out. Lifting my arms to cross them against my chest I wait with a glare steadied on the man before me. I arch a brow in question, when he realizes he has the floor he spills his secrets, which aren't even close to what I expect to hear.

"I have the flu; and I've had a fever for three days. I was so out of it when I woke up for my shift, I didn't realize I had taken the nighttime dose until it was too late." Rich's face is stained with tears as he explains himself. I rear back as his words sink in, the blade drops to the floor next to my feet. My blood boils in my veins as I stand in place for a moment.

"Are you fucking kidding me? You put her life at risk because you didn't want to use a goddamn sick day!" My words come out in a roar as I grip his throat again. His lips part as he attempts to grasp for air but this time there's no room for the fucker to breathe as I release my venomous words at him. "She could have been taken, or worse, you fucking idiot!"

Without another word I use my other hand to pull the gun from my waistband and place the muzzle into his open mouth and smile widely at the man in my grasp.

"No one will put her at risk again, motherfucker." I whisper into his ear before I look him square in the eyes and squeeze the trigger.

His head explodes in front of my eyes. Blood and brain matter land all over, including on my suit. Fuck, I forgot just how bloody this life is. I turn to face Milo and Michael. The latter is trying and failing to stifle his laughter. Milo on the other hand can't hide his anger.

"What the fuck, Johnny! He had the fucking flu." He snaps at me as I walk past him. "You could have done a fucking blood test to see if he was lying before you killed him. He was a good soldier!"

I feel the anger boiling under my skin again as I spin back around and step into Milo's space. He doesn't even flinch, good.

"Would you have waited around for a fucking test if someone tried to abduct my mother?" Milo takes a step back, startled at my accusation, but by the way he isn't arguing my point tells me all I need to know. "Yeah, that's what I thought – we'll be having a fucking conversation about that as soon as this cluster fuck of a situation is finished." I wave my hand over the direction of the body before I storm out. "Clean this shit up."

The steam from the shower envelopes me as I peel off the bloody clothes and leave them on the floor to dispose of later. As soon as I step inside, the water washes over my body and I press my forehead against the cool tile. Allowing myself a moment of calm before I face the woman that has had me twisted with so much sexual frustration since the day I met her it's not even funny. As I wash myself, my dick begins to stiffen with thoughts of her being pressed against me closer and closer each time we kiss. My hand wraps around the base and I squeeze myself, instantly appreciating the relief. Before I have a chance to continue, a loud scream startles me and I jump out of the shower nearly crashing into Nina who is standing in front of me with her eyes on the pile of bloody clothes on the floor. Fuck.

She rushes over to me; her hands find my forearms. She digs her nails in to keep me in place and looks up at my face, cataloging every part of me as water drips from my drenched, tousled hair. Her eyes well with unshed tears as she takes me in.

"What is it? What's wrong?" I ask as I take in her worried expression.

She meets my gaze and huffs out a heavy breath as she tries to explain why she barged into the bathroom.

"Pinhead was pawing at the door like he needed the litter box and when I opened it, I saw the clothes and I thought." She lets out a strained sob, "I thought something happened to you because of me." She tries to pull away as her gaze drops.

The moment she glances down to see the monster standing at full attention between my legs, she steps back with a pretty heat flushing her chest and neck. Nina spins away from me and I can't help but grin because I didn't miss the lust that filled her eyes before she turned her back to me. Her body is hidden under a thin tank top and a pair of sleep shorts that just barely cover her ass. Fuck, that is not helping the situation I desperately need to conceal. I grab the towel from the hook to my right and wrap it around my waist, a wasted attempt at hiding my erection. The tent between my legs is obvious as I step closer to her. My hands reach out and wrap around her middle as I press my lips to her ear which sends a shiver through her.

"I'm fine, *Bella*, it's not my blood." I chuckle at her body's reaction. "I had to," I weigh my options for a response before I finish. "Teach someone a lesson."

She whips around, her anxiety dissipates before my eyes; the fierce woman I saw earlier this evening has returned.

"Why do I feel that's not quite the truth?" Her brow arches as she glares at me. Her silver eyes are locked on mine as she studies me.

Chapter 22

Nina

I can't pull my gaze away from his warm chocolate stare. My heart beats frantically in my chest when I feel the tent of his towel inching closer to me the longer I stand in front of him. Giovanni smirks as I fight the urge to look down to what's between us.

"I had a," his lips twist into a maniacal smirk, "conversation with Rich." I cross my arms over my chest and keep my eyes trained on him as I silently wait for him to expand on what that means.

He chuckles and shakes his head before he divulges everything that happened after he left. My chest tightens, my hand flying up to my throat to clutch my imaginary pearls as he explains everything that he's done.

"Giovanni! Why would you?" I gasp, my eyes wide as I stare up at him while I try to comprehend what was just said, "You can't kill someone for having the flu! Why would you do that!?" My attempts at protesting his methods of dealing with Rich's mistake are dismissed as fast as they're spoken.

His fingers lift my chin when I try to look away right before his arms wrap tightly around my waist as he pulls me against him. His large hands press firmly against the small of my back. The hard rod between us presses against my stomach making me shiver with desire? Excitement? Fear? All of the above?

"*Bella*, the only way to show everyone just how serious I am about your safety is to make an example out of someone. Rich fucked up; he knew the risks." His hand lazily strokes up and down my spine, sending chills through me. "Had he informed one of us that he was sick, he would have been pulled from his station and Mrs. D would have likely made him soup and force fed him whatever magical concoction she can whip up to force out illness." We stare at each other for several seconds before he continues, "I will not apologize for making a point in claiming what's mine." Giovanni's declaration comes out in a growl, which sends a kaleidoscope of butterflies fluttering in my stomach.

My cheeks heat as my lips twitch, pulling into a smile no matter how much I attempt to fight the reaction.

"Yes, yours." I whisper as I lay my head against his chest. His arms tighten even more around me as we stand there for several seconds. I push back, pressing my palms against his damp chest. "I'll let you get back to your shower." I giggle as I unfold his arms from my waist and step out of his reach.

Giovanni's loud groan pulls my attention back to the direction of the shower. I swear I hear him mutter something about joining him, but by the time it registers he's back under the hot stream of water.

I pad over to find Pinhead sprawled on my side of the bed. He lifts his head as I pull the covers back and I swear, the damn cat rolls his eyes when I slide in. Rolls. His. Eyes. Can a cat even roll its eyes? Shaking my head at the idea, I take my spot. The luxurious feel of Giovanni's sheets against my thin pajamas sends a jolt of pleasure racing through my body.

I lay on my side as I stroke Pinhead's long fur while my other arm is tucked under the pillow. Memories of the last twenty-four hours flash through my mind's eye as I melt into the soft mattress. I never thought I'd have a first kiss, let alone a handful over a matter of hours. Every time he's kissed me it's felt like fireworks are exploding around us. It's everything I've always hoped for, yet like nothing I could have ever dreamed of. Knowing that I affect him enough to cause the type of reaction he's so clearly had around me, even if it terrifies me all the same, brings a smile to my face.

Irritation floods through me when light from the morning sun streams through the cracks in the blackout curtain which isn't doing enough to cover the large window across from our bed. When I try to stretch the sleep from my muscles, I realize strong arms have me caged in against a hot wall of muscle. I stiffen until I open my eyes and realize from the designs tattooed into the skin of the muscular forearms that are tight around my middle, I'm wrapped up in Giovanni.

My lips dance into a smile as I slide my body back closer into his. I wiggle as I relax back into him only to feel the stiff rod that was between us last night stabbing me in my ass. I swallow hard and try to tuck it behind me so I can get closer which only seems to make it angrier and harder. As I try to find comfort in his reaction to me, I feel his arm snake up between my breasts as he grips my neck before whispering in my ear.

"*Bella,* you're playing with fire, *amore.*" His voice is scratchy with sleep which does things to me I don't understand. "I've been barely holding myself back from taking you and filling you with every inch of me."

My brain misfires and I whimper, he somehow rolls me onto my back and lands on top of me in the blink of an eye. The amusement in his warm gaze has a fire heating between my legs. My lips part as he grinds his length against my core while he presses his lips to mine in a heated kiss. Our tongues tangle together as we greet each other after a night of sleep as if we hadn't just been wrapped up in one another. His hips press down a few more times which has a moisture pooling in my panties. What is happening to me?

"This is what you do to me, Nina." He groans into my neck before lifting his face to press another quick kiss to my lips. Giovanni is on his feet and in the bathroom before I have a chance to register what just happened.

Chapter 23
Nina

I'm sprawled out like a starfish on the bed, left with a dampness between my legs that has me feeling things I don't understand. There is an overwhelming feeling, a need at my center that I've never felt before. I press my legs together for some relief, the pressure feels like heaven, but I need more. More of what, I've yet to figure that out. I'm sitting with my back against the headboard with the covers wrapped tightly around my body to hide the moisture he caused. Not that he could see it unless he was between my legs, why does that thought make me even more excited?

Giovanni exits the bathroom, freshly showered, with just a pair of black boxer briefs covering him. My mouth dries at the sight. He's so beautiful, and I admire the black ink wraps like vines around every inch of his exposed skin. It ends at the wrist and is usually hidden when he's dressed in suits. The few times I've seen him in T-shirts or mostly bare like this, the beauty of his art steals my breath.

His lips twitch as a knowing grin pulls at the corner of his mouth. My eyes never leave his body while I watch him dress in his usual uniform of a fitted dark suit with a white button up underneath. He carefully secures a watch to his wrist before turning back to face me. The grin is even more apparent as Giovanni stalks toward my side of the bed. He leans forward and grabs hold of my ankles before dragging me to the edge. I let out a squeal at the sudden forced movement, which quickly turns into a giggle when he pulls me up into a seated position after I'm where he wants me.

"I'll see you tonight, Short Stack." His lips press against my forehead before he steps away with a wink that is sexier than should be legal.

Giovanni disappears from our room in a matter of seconds, and I'm left wondering with confusion clouding my every thought.

The rest of my morning is much the same between getting lost in a workout before a shower followed by breakfast with Vanna and Jade. Now though, I find myself in the living room curled up on a dark green chaise lounge with Pinhead purring against my chest while I read my favorite book. I've just reached the moment the female main character meets her love interest when I hear the clicking of heels against the hardwood floors.

"Hey Sweetheart, Tabatha will be here soon with her inventory." Vanna announces when enters the room, "What are you reading?" Her question is what pulls me from my book as she strolls closer to me.

After I explain a bit about the book I'm reading, she has a sour look twisting her face. She slides down to sit next to my legs as she pats my ankle gently before speaking.

"Sweetheart, you're how old?" Vanna's tone has my insides twisting in knots.

With my eyes trained on my hands I reply shyly, "I'll be twenty-five on October seventeenth."

Vanna's expression lightens, a bright smile takes over her face just as Tabatha walks in with several of Giovanni's men, Abel and Rand included. Racks and racks of clothes and boxes of shoes are brought in. My jaw drops wide as I see she in fact brought all of her inventory. Holy shit.

"Tabatha, you didn't have to actually bring *everything*! This is too much!" I exclaim as I jump to my feet and rush over to her. My arms wrap around her shoulders as soon as I reach her. "Thank you."

She waves her hand at me dismissively. "Oh dear, after what Janelle put you through, I will open a boutique in one of the extra bedrooms exclusively for you if you ask me to."

My eyes well with tears as I take my time to look at all that she's brought. I'm not sure how long I've been perusing when my arm begins to complain about the added weight. A giggle escapes when I realize I've loaded up on pieces I want to try on. Vanna has tears silently streaming down her cheeks that she tries to wipe away before I notice them as soon as I turn around.

"Is it ok?" I ask Tabatha who nods with a wink. Abel lifts the clothing from my arms and follows me to mine and Giovanni's room. He lays the pieces across the bed before disappearing back into the hall as he pulls the door closed behind him.

The next hour is spent as I would expect a nineties movie montage of wardrobe changes to happen. A number of jeans, dresses, tops, jackets, and shoes of every type are strewn about by the time I've finished and decided on what I want to keep. A handful of dresses that are much fancier than what I'm used to. Jeans that fit like a glove and a few shirts that show off my – uh, assets. I'm standing in front of a floor length mirror with a pair of red bottom platform boots. A tan exterior with a heel to give me some height but hopefully thick enough that I don't fall on my face.

I take a few unsteady steps across the length of the bedroom when I hear a gasp from the direction of the bedroom door. When I turn to find Vanna leaning in the doorway, I smile shyly unsure of what to say.

"Sweetheart, you look fantastic! You need those shoes. This entire outfit is absolutely you." She exclaims as she claps her hands excitedly and walks toward me to get a closer look at the dark wash blue jeans and purple cropped long sleeve shirt. It's cut in a low square showing off just enough of my chest that I feel sexy but not like I'm about to fall out of the top. A faux leather jacket over top finishes off the look. My cheeks flush as she spins me to get a full view.

"I feel good. I'm afraid I'm going to hurt myself in these shoes though. How do you walk in those?" I ask as I point to the thin stilettos she's always wearing.

She chuckles as she lifts her shoulders in a shrug.

"I know you had a rough first outing, but I have an idea." Vanna's smile is infectious, "You're going to be twenty-five in a week, yet you're still reading a book for teenagers. Would you like to go to a small bookstore with me? We can find you something more age appropriate." Her lips turn up into a wicked grin as I cross my arms over my chest to protect myself. "I promise you, Sweetheart; I won't be out of earshot, and I know damn well after how you spoke to Tabs, you've got a handle on your emotions enough to fuck someone up if they speak to you inappropriately."

My jaw drops for the second time today before my shock turns into a fit of laughter. She leads me out to say goodbye to Tabatha, who is just as giddy as Vanna was over my style choices.

Abel pulls the SUV up outside of the bookstore, Under the Cover. My eyes go wide when I get a glimpse of the inside. I follow Vanna quickly as soon as she opens the car door. Abel and Rand are barely out of their seats by the time I've reached the entrance. A staccato rhythm beats in my chest as soon as I step through the threshold to find a woman with a radiant smile behind the counter.

"Hi! Welcome to Under the Cover, I'm Brittany. Let me know if you need help finding anything!" She announces just before Vanna joins me. She's beautiful, she's got a wild air about her with beautiful tattoos covering every piece of skin that's on display, and that's most of it given she's wearing a fitted tank top with a mini skirt. The ink on her legs is obscured a tad by the fishnet stockings, but just a little. You can still see the beauty with the little bit that's hidden.

"Hey, Sweetheart, how have you been?" Vanna walks to the counter where Brittany steps around to greet her with a warm hug. She's adorable, her hair is dark with a bright pink ombre effect. Her makeup is flawless, a peachy eyeshadow makes her hazel eyes pop. They stop me where I am several yards away.

"V! I haven't seen you in months." She exclaims as soon as she gets her arms around Vanna.

The two of them begin chatting while I look around. Just taking time to appreciate my surroundings. I'm living my best Belle fantasy life when I see the wooden ladder that slides along the wall. There are several reading nooks plus a swing with silk flowers and vines wrapped around the ropes that tether it to the ceiling. I spin when I register someone approaching my side.

"Hi! It's so nice to meet you. Vanna said that you love to read, but you've not been able to get anything new for a while. I'd love to help." Brittany's confidence has my brain whirling.

I take a step back as I suck in a deep breath to center myself. She's not threatening, she's just friendly. It's fine, I'm fine.

"Yeah, I've not had," I pause, contemplating my next words. "I've not had access to anything new for quite some time. I got a hold of a book by an author a while ago that was well, hot. But, I forget the name of it."

Her already bright smile has turned into a wicked grin mirroring one I've seen from Giovanni. Vanna is acting interested in whatever book she picked up, but I can see the smile in her eyes from where I stand. Traitor.

"Oh, Tink – we're going to get real close, real fast." Brittany giggles as she talks faster than I've ever heard someone speak. "Tell me everything about you. What are your kinks? Your likes, dislikes? We'll start with something that you actually enjoy and branch out from there."

My cheeks heat and I look anywhere but at the other people in the store. This is embarrassing!

"I uh – I don't know." I admit as I allow my hair to fall in front of my face like a curtain.

She wraps her arm around my shoulder as she directs me toward a wall of books, "You're vanilla. That's fine, let's see."

"What? No, I mean, I've never –" The words die on my tongue as soon as I realize she understands.

"Oh. My. God! A virgin! Miss ma'am, this is going to be fun!" She squeals as she spins me in the complete opposite direction toward a different wall of books as she points out her favorite books for beginners.

Giddiness floods my veins as I observe the scene before me. Michael slices into the torso of one of Mr. Barone's dealers. Loud wails sound from the man who clearly never expected his chosen profession to land him in this situation. What a pity, most people who get into illegal dealings know their death will likely be a painful one.

"I didn't ask for this! They forced me to do it!" He exclaims as his chest rises and falls with heavy breaths.

Michael takes a step back and glances over his shoulder at me. A silent conversation passes between us. He doesn't trust the man and quite honestly neither do I, but I nod allowing him to take a break while I join in on the interrogation.

"Who forced you?" The man whose name I've already forgotten stares up at me with wide eyes as I wait for a response.

He blinks rapidly before speaking, "Frederico and Mateo. They told me if I didn't they'd kill my wife." The man's eyes are filled with fear, which you'd expect, but something is missing.

I stand in front of him pondering his statement for several minutes. He becomes more anxious the longer I remain unmoving and silent. His already ghostly white skin pales even more when I step back to allow Michael access again.

"The thing is, even if Mateo and Frederico have forced you, I know for a fact that you aren't married." I bark out as I fight laughter, "Besides, if you were in fact uninterested in this lifestyle, you would have been in contact as soon as word got out that I had taken over for my grandfather."

The fear that had been in his eyes dissipates as quickly as it came, replaced by rage. I snort when he tries to fight the restraints and nod to Michael who has been waiting for an all clear. He lifts his blade to the man's throat before he leans in, obscuring my view and murmuring the threat that usually does it for these pieces of shit. Just like clockwork, he sings like a canary.

"All I know is that Frederico went to Barone a few years ago. Word on the street, at the time, was that Ludovico was losing power. I don't know anything else, I swear!" The admission comes out in a breathy sob.

The confession has me pause as I consider his words. Part of the paperwork I found did give a hint to that. However, by the look in the man's eyes, he has no other information. I shrug and give the signal to Michael who pulls his gun from his holster and pulls the trigger. A loud shot rings through the small space as the man slumps over. His brain matter and skull fragments blown onto the wall behind him.

Michael's call to the cleanup crew is swift; by the time he's changed and thrown his clothes in the incinerator, they're already here. I have no idea how they do it, but they're fast as fuck. We leave them to it and head back to the car where Milo is on watch. As soon as I slide into the front passenger seat, he shoots me the goofiest grin.

"The fuck is wrong with your face?" I glance between him and Michael who looks just as concerned.

Milo chuckles at our reaction.

"Nina is out of the house with Vanna." His tone is that of a proud father. Given that he's the one who quite literally rescued her from the hell she was in and saw first-hand just how sheltered and frightened she was in those first precious moments, I'm not surprised. Although, the fact that she's out without me has my heart stuttering in my chest.

My vision blurs to a red haze as I point for him to drive.

"Get me to wherever the fuck they are, now." I demand.

Milo doesn't move but I feel his eyes on me.

"Johnny, man — she's got Vanna and her two men with them." He tries to soothe the panic by reassuring me of her safety, which isn't doing a goddamn thing. "They're at a bookstore. They're fine."

"Drive." I repeat through a guttural growl.

The last time she was out, someone was such a dick to her that she couldn't function for hours. There's no way I'm going to allow that to fucking happen again. I have to be there for her, to protect her.

I step through the front door of Under the Cover to find my mother leaning against the counter speaking with an employee who looks bored out of their mind. My mother eyes me the moment I enter, and she's got a shit eating grin splitting her face. She's proud of herself. Oh, we'll be talking later. Even if I'm proud of the woman who made such huge progress today, I don't like that I wasn't made aware of this outing before it happened.

It only takes a moment for my eyes to land on my woman. She's dressed in a pair of jeans that make her ass look even better than usual. Seriously, I could bounce a quarter off that perfect peach. She has a black leather jacket draped over her arm, I can see the lower half of her back with the short purple top she's wearing. Fuck, barely anything is exposed, and yet, I would kill for a moment alone with her.

There's another woman whose arm is wrapped tight around Nina's shoulder; her bright pink hair bounces around frantically in her ponytail as she talks with her hands. She steps away from Nina to move to the counter, I take that as my moment to swoop in and wrap my arms around Nina's chest. I just nearly miss the collection of books in her hand. She stiffens for a second, until I speak softly against her ear.

"You look good enough to eat, Short Stack." My words calm her and she melts into me.

The woman with pink hair walks back to Nina who is still in my arms and takes the stack from her.

"Thanks, Brittany." Nina's appreciation seems to be deeper than for the books. I'm going to have some questions about that later.

Before Brittany walks away she says loud enough for both of us to hear, "Tink, you are for sure going to be graduating sooner than you think." The pink haired woman winks at me before she disappears behind the counter to ring up the books.

My mother is off to the side having a hushed conversation with Milo which only serves as a point of contention, so I do my best to ignore them. Michael is at the counter with his wallet out before I can make a move.

Brittany's eyes roam up Michael's body as soon as she realizes it's someone new at the counter. Her eyes flicker with mischief as her mouth opens.

"Well hello there, Daddy." Her voice is full of lust.

Michael's face flames at the forwardness of the young woman. She's so close to Nina's age I choke back a laugh, burying my face in Nina's neck as I direct her outside with me.

We've spent the last twenty-four hours combing through every piece of paperwork that Frederico left in this house. I'm exhausted and infuriated. I lift my head to see Milo going line by line on the current stack in front of him. Michael lets himself back in my office with a fresh round of coffee. The fragrance of Mrs. D's dark roast fills the room and a jolt of energy hits before I even get my first sip. Milo snorts when I leap from my seat to grab a cup. The steaming liquid hits my tongue, and I flinch at the heat. I don't even care, it's doing its job of waking me up. Bring on the pain.

"I don't understand why the money that is supposed to be allocated to help those coming into the city for a better life legally and safely has dwindled so much." I groan through gritted teeth. "This was agreed upon years ago, back when Frederico started accepting payment from the corrupt fucks at City Hall for protection from anyone digging into their extracurricular activities." My tired eyes rake through another page of data, and I let out a long huff. All of these numbers and words are blurring together.

Everything points to Barone, as it has since we began this wild fucking goose chase. The math isn't mathing because how he became so entwined with our business, illegitimate and legal ventures alike, doesn't make sense. There's no fucking way that millions of dollars a year are going out for drug distribution. We should be in the goddamn black tenfold with how much cocaine and heroin go for on the streets.

The more time we spend trying to figure out when it happened and what started it, the angrier I feel. Anger radiates through me as I re-read the same line for the third goddamn time.

"We need to get this figured the fuck out and back to taking care of the people of this fucking town." My words come out jumbled into a growl and snarl. I stand and begin to pace the length of the office weaving between the piles of paperwork that are strewn about.

I throw myself back onto my chair when something catches my eye, but before I have a chance to register what it could mean there's a loud bang on the office door, Danny Boy comes tumbling in, clearly in a panic. I cock a brow at the soldier who has been an integral part of my team since I've returned home. He's never one to burst in so it's obvious to anyone who pays attention that this is serious.

"Sorry to interrupt, boss. There's chatter on the street that Barone is claiming you've abducted Nina and are holding her captive." He explains, rushing through his words. "He's trying to recruit more people to come in at night. One of my men heard it down at the barbershop. They didn't realize who he was."

My blood turns molten in my veins, fury ready to explode on this motherfucker. In a heartbeat, Nina appears in the doorway. She's dressed in a tight pair of yoga pants that show off every curve and what looks like one of my dark hoodies, which thankfully, covers her assets. The expression on her face tells me she heard exactly what was said. What her father is claiming.

"I'm not a fucking pawn!" She screams so loudly the windows practically rattle in their frames. Her feet are planted in place where she stands just inside the doorway glaring at me. She's got a book in her hand hanging by her side. I cock a brow when I see a half-naked man on the cover. A mixture of curiosity and jealousy begin to take over, but before I can make a comment, she breaks the silence. "Take me out. If we're seen in public, anyone who is concerned will be able to tell I'm not a prisoner, that I'm perfectly happy here. With you."

Her determination and confidence is sexy as sin. I'm not sure where it's come from, but fuck me. I cross my arms against my broad chest as I keep my eyes trained on her. Nothing about her body language tells me she's afraid. She's pissed and ready to bring hell to earth. Just the thought of her ready to set fire to anyone who stands in her way has my heart pumping with pride.

"While I would love to have you on my arm, are you sure you're ready for that, *Bella*? If we do this I can't call in a favor to force limited seating. We'd have to go with no buffer." I urge her to consider everything before making a decision.

"No, but I'm done being treated as his possession. Plus, you're not leaving my side this time." The confidence and determination she's got on display has my dick stiff as stone.

I keep my mask of indifference in place and snap at the men to get out and close the door. The three of them rush out and comply, leaving the two of us alone. It's not lost on me that this is the first time I haven't asked her if I can close the door, but right now I can't share her attention.

I hook my finger and motion for her to come closer. She stalks toward me, like a lioness ready to pounce on her prey, but before she can, I wrap my arm around her waist and drag her into me. My lips crash against her soft pout. My tongue dips into her mouth savoring every soft whimper and moan. I tease her tongue the way I want to tease other parts, which has her moaning louder as she melts against my chest. Her body is pliant, ready, and willing to do anything I please. I chuckle as I pull away, knowing I need to give the power back to her. She whines in protest when I don't go back in for another kiss, her beautiful silver eyes imploring me to take it further.

"I'll do anything for you, Short Stack." My lips twist into a grin before I press another soft kiss to her forehead.

Chapter 26

Nina

I texted Brittany a few hours ago to tell her about my date. I have a date. She insisted that she come over to help me get ready. While I'm grateful, it's a little unnerving to have someone outside of Vanna and Jade care so much to be there for me when it comes to Giovanni and me. Dinner isn't for a couple of hours, so after I took her on a tour of the house, we've been huddled up in the living room enjoying silent company while we read our books. She's reading a romance involving the mafia which made me giggle when she told me about it. I worry something like that would hit too close to home for me. I'm content with the small-town virgin book she suggested for me.

A throat clearing pulls my attention from the book right when the main characters were getting close, and the interruption annoys me. I look up to find Jade watching us with a warm smile on her lips. She takes a step into the living room before she speaks.

"You may want to start getting ready, dear. Johnny asked Abel to drive you to the restaurant in an hour and a half." She chirps before disappearing back into the enormous house.

Brittany leaps from the couch and claps her hands together like a toddler finding out they get a cookie after naptime. Her fingers lock with mine as she pulls me to my feet and drags me to my room. She all but shoves me into the shower declaring she will find an outfit for me while I'm getting cleaned up.

"Do I really need to shave –" I cut myself off embarrassed that this is a conversation, "there?"

Brittany's infectious laugh makes me feel a bit lighter.

"Yes babe, trust me. When you finally get that man to nail you to the bed, it's going to be so much better if you're bald." She sounds giddy on my behalf, which just makes me giggle as I step under the hot stream of the water.

I make quick work of washing up and shaving everything I've been told to. A shiver runs through my body when my hand sweeps over my bare pussy as I towel myself off. Jesus, has it always been so sensitive?

When I step out onto the cool tile floor, I notice a small pile of black fabric laying on the counter. I tip toe toward it, nervous about what I'm about to find. A smile dances on my lips when I see a beautiful lace bra, which I easily pull on, but pause when I see what looks like a lace string.

"What the hell is this?" I squeak, Brittany's head pops through the cracked bathroom door with a wicked smile.

"Trust me, you'll both appreciate this." She chuckles before she vanishes.

A groan passes my lips as I pull on the tiny underwear. As soon as I have them in place I notice an even more sensational pleasure against my clit. Seriously? What the hell am I doing? I softly whimper into the towel annoyed and frustrated with the reaction my body is having to not having a barrier of hair between my legs.

I step out into the bedroom and find that Brittany has a black dress that I chose from Tabatha pulled and ready for me. As soon as she sees me she motions for me to spin back around and go into the bathroom. She follows me inside with bags of new makeup that she picked up for me. A lone tear streaks down my cheek, I wipe it away trying to avoid the emotion this gesture is causing.

She spends an hour between my makeup and hair. By the time I have the dress and high heels on, that she insisted on despite my hesitancy, I look unrecognizable. An audible gasp escapes when I look in the floor length mirror.

"Britt, I – you did this?" I stare in awe at the woman looking back at me in the mirror.

My face still has my natural look but everything is accentuated in the best way, while the biggest difference is the red that has been painted on my lips.

"Laney Boggs wishes she looked this good," She grins at my reflection knowing my love for *She's All That.*

I turn and fling myself against my friend, with the magic she created today I feel like an entirely different person. I finally have a friend.

My eyes are locked on my fingers tangled together in my lap as I wait for the car door to be opened. Anxiousness has been crawling through my veins since I got in the car, unsure of how Giovanni is going to react to how I look. What if he doesn't like it? Before I have a chance to spiral even further into my own thoughts, the door opens, exposing me to the outside world. My first real public outing. Abel steps close to help me out, a knowing grin on his stupid face.

"He's going to love it, take a deep breath because he's on the other side of the door." Abel doesn't try to stifle his laughter as he pushes the door closed behind me.

I turn around slowly and see Giovanni standing with a group of people a few paces away. His gaze lifts to find me. His eyes go wide and his demeanor changes. Without finishing his conversation, he steps away and makes his way to me. A look I saw the other morning is in his eyes, and my cheeks flush at the memory.

"*Bella,* you look..." he doesn't finish as his eyes rake up and down my body. I feel my chest and cheeks flame as he makes his interest so publicly known. He shakes his head and leans in, pressing his lips to my ear before quietly murmuring "*Amore mio, stasera mi costringerai a uccidere qualcuno.*"

My body goes still as I jerk back with an unspoken question in my wide gaze. The lessons his mom and Jade have been giving me allow me to pick out pieces of that. He's going to kill someone? He chuckles before explaining "You don't realize just how tempting you are, *Bella.*"

His eyes crease in the corners as his smile becomes wicked before he leans in and presses his mouth to my red painted lips, with no care in the word. Thankfully, Brittany got me a transfer proof lipstick. My body becomes pliant as I melt into him ready to take everything he's willing to give. A low growl escapes the man who has my full attention just before he pulls away. My eyes flutter open to see Abel standing next to him with an amused expression, gesturing to us that we need to enter the restaurant.

"Are you sure you're ready for this?" Giovanni's warm chocolate eyes send my heart bouncing around in my chest. The way this man cares for me will never be something I get used to.

My hands loop around Giovanni's bicep as I nod, "I know you won't let anyone hurt me. Right now, I'm more worried about falling in these shoes." I giggle as we walk together into the classy establishment.

As soon as the hostess sees Giovanni, her demeanor changes slightly as she presses her breasts together and leans in toward him to show off her cleavage. I arch a perfectly manicured brow – thank you Britt – at the exchange. He doesn't seem to notice her behavior as we follow the woman to our table. After he pulls out my chair to help me take my seat, I place my hands on the table, while I watch the scene unfold before me. She places her hand on his forearm and begins to lean into him again, as if she's going to speak into his ear.

"Excuse me, ma'am." I call for the woman's attention as sweetly as I can muster in my irritated state. "Do you paw at all of your guests this way or only the patrons who are so obviously on a date?"

Giovanni chokes on the water he just lifted to his lips at my directness. The hostess stammers out a pathetic apology before she rushes back to her station. When my eyes land on his face, I'm greeted by the most beautiful smile. His eyes sparkle with pride as he places his hand over mine, squeezing gently.

"*Bella*, no one holds a candle to you." He chuckles reassuringly.

My shoulders drop as I let out the breath I'd been holding in an attempt to center myself and not use some of the moves Giovanni has been teaching me on the woman. When I don't reply right away, his hand squeezes mine again.

"It doesn't mean that I'm ok with her touching what's mine." I roll my eyes, unable to hide my annoyance.

The eyes of every person in the restaurant land on us at one point or another while we're enjoying our meal over conversation. A few people even approach and introduce themselves as Giovanni's colleagues. I just smile and nod while shaking hands with men who look like older versions of my father.

The drive back to Ludovico Estate ends too quickly. Giovanni's hand lays on top of my thigh with his thumb caressing my bare skin the entire drive. I feel so amped up I inwardly groan when we arrive back at the house. While I may be grateful to be in a safe space of solitude for a while. Ok, not complete solitude, but at least people I know. As soon as we step through the entryway he presses me against the wall, his mouth lands on mine. My lips part in a gasp at the sudden connection, and he wastes no time sliding his tongue inside. His expert tongue explores my mouth like we hadn't just kissed a few hours ago.

The moment he sucks on my tongue, I moan and melt into him, my hands loop around his neck and I let go of everything as we take the time for ourselves. This is the first moment we've been alone since seeing one another tonight. That is until the clicking of heels sound against the hardwood floor inching closer to us. He pulls away and groans as his mother appears from the direction of the living room.

"Oh, good! It looks like you two are having a great night. I was just heading to bed." Her infectious grin is one I've seen before when we had our talk in the garden. I shake my head and bury my face in Giovanni's chest.

"Goodnight, Mother." He groans as the sound of her steps sound further in the distance. "Let's get to bed." His tone changes to something warmer when he speaks to me.

When we get back to our room, he kicks off his shoes into the corner while I stand unsure of what to do. He presses a soft kiss to my forehead before telling me he's going to get a shower before he lays down. Still in a daze as he disappears into the bathroom I find my way to the bed and sit down with my back against the headboard.

I pick up the book I had been reading earlier and dive back in. There's an entire chapter dedicated to the male character burying his face between the female characters legs and the thought has me squirming. I flip the page to find that she's had another orgasm when a low growl startles me from the story.

"What are you reading, Short Stack?" Giovanni asks, he's leaning against the side of the bed, his eyes trained on the paperback book in my hands. His bare chest on full display with water droplets cascading down his dewy skin. I glance down to find he's only in a towel. My throat bobs as I swallow hard at the sight before me.

"Oh, it's just a book that Brittany recommended." I murmur as I cross my arms over my chest hiding the cover from him.

His brow arches as he sits on the bed next to me.

"It must be pretty damn exciting, because I can smell your arousal from here." His lips turn up into a wicked smirk.

"Wait, what? I smell? What do you mean I smell!" My eyes widen as I scramble closer to the headboard, dragging my knees into my chest.

Giovanni's deep chuckle reverberates through the room landing directly between my legs. What. The. Fuck. He crawls up the bed, the towel still snug around his waist though I can see it pitched like a fucking tent again. His lips find mine, the tension in my body seeming to dissipate the moment he swipes his tongue against my lips, teasing me.

"*Amore mio*, it's not a bad thing. You smell delicious." His face dips to my neck where he sucks gently at a spot just behind my ear causing my back to arch into him. He lifts his face to mine before speaking again. "May I taste you?"

I don't know how to form words. My gaze travels to the book which he moved to the bedside table and back to him as he continues to trail kisses down my chest. My every nerve ending feels like it's on fire. Giovanni's eyes lock on mine as he slides the strap of my black dress and down my shoulders just enough to yank down the top, exposing the lace bra my friend chose. A low growl rumbles up his chest as he dips his fingers into the cups to yank them down. Giovanni sucks in a breath when he sees my breasts for the first time. My nipples pebble so tight it's almost painful until his mouth latches on, sucking the peaked tip so hard I feel my legs begin to tremble. I become frustrated when he pulls back until he latches onto the next one, only to leave me on the edge again.

"Giovanni!" I cry out between pants as he pulls me down a bit further onto the bed.

He grins up at me as he trails kisses down my abdomen over the material of the dress until he carefully tugs up so that my thong covered pussy is exposed, the dress now only covering my midsection.

My lips quiver as he dips his head down and breathes in the scent of my most private part over my panties before he gingerly pulls them down. His lips press soft wet kisses up my thighs, the scruff of his short facial hair against the sensitive skin feels better than I would have imagined. He whispers something I can't quite hear a second before I feel him connect to me. The sensation of his practiced tongue swiping up my juices makes my body convulse. He chuckles which only makes it worse as the vibrations against my clit send me to the moon and back.

My chest heaves as I pant through the return to earth. Unable to form a sentence or express anything at this time, I prop myself up on my elbows to look down at the god between my legs who is staring back up at me with a wicked grin. Giovanni winks at me before he lowers his mouth back to my pussy, causing me to collapse back onto the bed.

A symphony consisting solely of my moans and whimpers of pleasure echoes around the room as he repeatedly swirls his tongue around my clit finding the spot over and over again that feels so fucking good I can't see straight.

"Gio-God," my moans are a strangled whimper at this point as he sucks my clit between his lips in a rhythm of rapid succession that has me seeing stars for the third time. He must sense I can't take any more because he crawls back up my body, evidence of my arousal and release from my first three orgasms glisten on his face as he presses his lips to mine.

I drag my hand through his hair, holding him in place so I can get my fill of him. He groans, a sound filled with pain before he backs away.

"I'll be back in a few minutes, I need to," a pregnant pause passes before he continues. "I need to take care of something."

My curiosity and unwillingness to be apart from him right now win out, and I speak before I can chicken out.

"Wait, can I...watch?" I ask, stumbling over the last word.

Giovanni's eyelids are heavy with lust as he observes me for a moment before making the decision. He nods and sits back against the headboard. I scoot back to be able to watch from a comfortable position next to him. He unhooks the towel exposing himself to me. I gasp seeing it so close, yet afraid to get too close. It's so long and thick, but the smooth skin is so beautiful. His hand wraps around the base, squeezing firmly before stroking to the tip. I gasp when I notice the bead of liquid pooling at the top, but I don't want to distract him to ask any questions right now. I can feel his eyes locked on me as he continues to stroke himself. The muscles in his thighs go rigid as his breaths become more ragged. I whimper as I watch, caught up in the lust of seeing this man bring himself pleasure. Realizing that pleasure because of me is almost too much. The whimper must have been too much for him because I notice his abs flex just as his hips jerk up into his fist as ropes of a creamy liquid shoot out of his cock and land on his stomach. His head drops back against the pillow as he lets out a satisfied "Fuck!"

Without thinking, I reach over and swipe my finger through his release and bring it to my lips. My mouth wraps around my finger before licking it clean. I groan, he tastes so good. It's unlike anything I've ever tasted before, but I need more.

Johnny

Beads of sweat drip down my face as I face off against one of my enforcers. His mean mug would terrify anyone else but me, I'm used to it. I fake left when Michael attempts to swing on me. My lips dance while I fight back a grin as I wind my arm back and throw a punch, only for him to duck just before impact. I stumble forward a few steps before I find my footing again. An exasperated grunt escapes as I regain my concentration. I turn back to face him and he's laughing maniacally, his face filled with more amusement than I'd expect from a man who is more dangerous than the guy from Hellraiser. *What was his name?*

"I've missed this, my free time has been spent training Nina. I haven't had a chance to work up a sweat in a while." The comment passes my lips as I dance around him on the mat. His brow arches mocking me from a few paces away.

The smartass expression on his face triggers something inside me and I lunge forward, my left arm winding back only to swing forward fast to land hard against the side of his face. Michael, a man who has killed so many people the number is unknown, stands straight, not being affected by the impact. His Cheshire grin taunts me as an uncertainty about my boxing capabilities clouds my confidence.

"That punch was weak, you're holding back." He stifles a laugh before continuing, "Quit being a bitch, just because I'm older than you doesn't mean I can't take a hit."

If my glare could shoot bullets, this man would be riddled with holes. He's so amused with himself he's bouncing on his toes motioning for me to come at him again. So, in an attempt to take him off his game, I throw a taunt back at him.

"Oh, ok. Daddy." My mouth turns up into a smirk as I throw another punch to the left side of his face followed closely with a jab to his nose sending him backward. I snort out a laugh as he nearly lands on his ass before he plants his feet back into the ground again. "What the hell was that about anyway?"

Michael wipes a hand down his face and shakes his head. He bends down to grab a bottle of water as his face flushes to a shade of red that would make the Looney Tunes proud. He takes his time sipping the drink. The fucker loves to mess with me. Once he places the drink back on the ground at the edge of the mat he glares at me.

"No fucking clue, man, I've never seen the girl before." His shoulders lift and drop in a noticeable shrug. "Even when your mother would frequent the place before you returned, Milo was the one who would accompany her."

I shudder before walking up to Michael and sending a jab into his kidney, his body bends in half as he holds his side coughing as he tries to catch his breath.

"That's for making me think about the two of them after she reads those books." I gag dramatically which only makes him laugh through the attempt to breathe.

He stands back to his full height towering over me as we go a few more rounds. The man is quick on his feet and I end up stumbling more than I land hits. The last round he fakes right before dropping to the ground and sweeps my legs out from under me. Laughter erupts from my chest as soon as I land on my ass. Michael holds out a hand to help me back to my feet which I happily accept and clap his shoulder in thanks.

"Jesus, old man. Maybe I should have you train Nina." I brush my hands over my ass to make sure there's no dust or dirt on them from the ground.

My world turns upside down as I'm lifted into the air and my body is slammed back onto the ground with Michael standing over me, a scowl on his face. He holds his hand out to me to help me back up as he explains himself. "That's for calling me an old man. I'll train her, but she'll be able to easily take your ass down a few pegs when I'm done with her."

I roll my neck, not accepting his help this time, I stand back up on my own. Instinctively, I take a few steps away from him so he can't knock me down again. Our gazes lock for a moment as his seriousness sinks in.

"If she can take me, then I'll be less worried about anyone else getting ahold of her." I admit, my tone grim. The fact of the matter is, I don't trust that her father won't send anyone else for her and that scares the shit out of me because I can't be by her side twenty-four-seven. Knowing she'll have Michael's training in her back pocket gives me a sense of relief that I hadn't realized I've been needing.

Chapter 28
Nina

My eyes roam the shelves of the newest releases and new inventory that Brittany has on the shelves. The past few days have been quite predictable, which I appreciate. Most of my free time is spent here at the bookstore whenever Brittany is working, so I can slowly get used to new people without large crowds and loud noises. I pause when I see a familiar cover, *Matched with a Billionaire* by Sara Hurst. I squeal to myself as I pull it off the shelf. It's been so long since I read this book, but since it was the first *adult* romance that I had ever read, I have to get it. That's like a rule or something, right?

"Are you ok over there?" Britt asks as she looks up from where she stands behind the counter typing away on the computer.

I grin and nod as I continue to peruse the section. Only a minute passes when a hand darts out in front of me, frantically turning me around. I gasp, relaxing only when I realize that it's my friend, just acting strange. My eyes go wide as she stares at me without speaking a word. Brittany's jaw drops and she screams out an unintelligible cheer.

"That man rocked your world! Tell me everything!" She exclaims as she links my fingers with hers and drags me over to a sitting area.

"Uhh – I don't – uhh." I stutter as my eyes dart around the store. Abel and Rand are standing so close I know they can hear everything based on the way Abel is choking on laughter. I hope he chokes on his damn tongue.

He must recognize my annoyance with his big brotherly – or at least what I assume is a big brotherly reaction to my embarrassment. Abel claps Rand on his shoulder and drags him as far away as he can to give us some space. Once they're far enough away that I feel comfortable continuing this conversation, I turn back to face my friend.

"You're glowing, I need the tea!" She giggles, clapping her hands together in excitement like she had before my date a few days ago. I smile, shaking my head at her before I lower my voice and go into detail.

We spend a few minutes delving into my first orgasm experience and her eyes nearly rolled into the back of her head when I told her I swiped his cum from his stomach to taste it. *"That's so fucking hot!"* is scream whispered at me as she glances over her shoulder at my shadows.

My smile grows wider the more we talk. I love having someone to talk about anything to.

"It was like the book came to life as I was reading it." My cheeks heat as I recall the events of our first time together. He's made it his mission to start every morning and end every night between my thighs since that first night. "The main male character had just done the same thing in the book when Giovanni made the move. I was so overwhelmed after. I felt like I wanted to do more, but had no idea where to start." My confession lifts something from my chest I didn't realize has been weighing on me.

Another squeal sounds as Brittany jumps to her feet before lowering herself back down next to me. She leans in to make sure no one else can hear whatever the hell is about to come out of her mouth. Her lips turn up into a mischievous grin before she speaks.

"You need to work on your endurance." She motions a dick going into her mouth and I lift my hands to my mouth in shock. She did not just do that! "You don't want to have it in your mouth and only be able to keep him there for a few seconds before your jaw tightens. So, we practice!" She talks with her hands, her voice increasing in volume the more excited she gets at her idea. "My shift ends in ten minutes; do you think your boy toys over there would drive us to another store?"

My body goes rigid at the thought. I've yet to feel entirely comfortable anywhere but here since having freedom. I glance over to the men, my throat bobs as I swallow hard trying to think of how to get out of this. I decide on honesty.

"I don't see why not, but, I don't know that being around a lot of people is a good idea for me." I admit as I twist my fingers in my lap.

Brittany's smile is infectious and she boops me on the nose. I arch a brow at her which just makes her giggle.

"Don't worry, Tink, there's rarely a crowd where we're going." She jumps up from her seat leaving me on my own again before she turns around. "That book is on me by the way."

Thirty-five minutes later Brittany is in the back seat of Abel's SUV directing him on which way to go. She has refused to just give them the name of the establishment so that they can look up the address, but she's being stubborn. Her insistence on a surprise has me both curious and anxious to find out what she's got planned.

When we arrive outside of a building with blacked out windows and neon lights that flash the words "Adult gifts," my blood runs cold. Abel begins to giggle as he and Rand step out of the car. A moment later they're opening the back doors to let us out and Rand holds out a hand to help me step down, his mask of indifference is in place and I'm so thankful for it.

We round the back of the SUV to find Abel still giggling like a teenager as we approach. I shove him in the chest which only seems to make the man laugh harder.

"How the hell am I supposed to face these two after I go in here?" I whisper to Brittany who is grinning ear to ear as she looks at me.

Her ease about being here should make me feel more comfortable, but Giovanni not being here is what fills me with unease.

"Do you actually care about them or your man in this scenario?" Her words hit home and she knows it, she giggles and claps her hands together again as I gesture for her to lead the way.

I feel the impact in my bones as I slam my fist into the latest in a long line of fuck nuggets that we have to get through. His blood splatters across my face when I release another punch straight into his nose, which will most definitely never be straight again. Not that it will matter after this.

At this point, I'm simply taking my frustration and anger out on the man. We've been going at this for weeks, since I brought Nina into my home, which is why I'm so fucking pissed. When he gave her to me without a second thought or taking a moment to consider what I could do to her – not that I'd do anything she hasn't asked for, he signed his death certificate.

I roll my neck working out some of the kinks before I pull my knife from my pocket and slice him open. He's given us everything he can or will, so he's useless to us. Just my play toy.

A loud ding sounds from behind me interrupting my train of thought. Only two people have access to get through my do not disturb when I'm working in these situations. I turn to face Michael who has my phone in his hand reading what was sent.

"You may want to clean up before we leave, there is something more important for us to do." His brow arches as he stares at me from where he remains leaning against the wall. His large arms folded across his chest. A knowing smile plastered on his smug face.

The text from my mother wasn't necessarily urgent, however I'm happy to have seen it with time to run a few errands before my attendance is required at home. Michael pulls the SUV up to the spot just outside Oopsie Daisy, a local florist that most people's go to for forgotten celebrations. However, the place is run by my aunt on my dad's side, who I haven't seen in years.

The exterior looks exactly the same as the last time I had been here before leaving. My heart skips a beat as I step out of the car when I see a tall woman with short grey hair through the window. She's twelve years older than my mom, but looks damn good for her age. Time has treated her well. My aunt Celeste smiles while she helps a customer. My eyes find Michael, who nods for me to go in alone. I pull open the door, the scent of fresh flowers engulfing me in a cloud causing a flood of memories to return like a slap in the face.

"Best of luck, Sweetheart, let me know if you need another bouquet. Forgetting your first wedding anniversary usually requires some jewelry too." She reaches across the counter and places her hand on the customer's hand to offer sympathy before offering a card with the other. "Go here and ask for Joe, he'll help you find something."

The customer repeatedly thanks her as they walk past me and out the door. Her green eyes raise to meet mine and I smirk as soon as the recognition clicks. She rushes around the counter, her eyes sparkle as she moves toward me, I take a few steps to shorten the distance. I feel her shoulders shake with quiet sobs when she crashes into me, and my arms fold tight around her tiny frame.

"Hey, Auntie C." I chuckle through bleary eyes.

She pulls away to cup my hands between her aged hands, the only part of her that looks visibly older. She presses a kiss to each side of my face before speaking.

"Child! Don't you dare Auntie C me. It's been eight years since you've let me see you!" She shakes her head at me. "I have missed you so damn much kid! Your Uncle Joe will be so happy to know you are home!"

She and Joe are the only two people I've stayed in contact with. They tend to make an annual trip to the Philadelphia Flower Show. She's attended design classes and even taught a few over the years while they've attended. I may have joined them every year up until I opened my own firm. My aunt may be an understanding person, but she's given me shit about it as often as she can get in touch with me.

"Will you ever let me off the hook? I'm back and you'll see me as often as you'd like now." I chuckle as I press a kiss against her cheek.

She swats my chest as she drags me over to behind the counter so we can sit on the stools she has hidden back there. I shake my head with a small smile, this place hasn't changed at all.

"I figured I'd see you at some point when I heard about him." She cocks a brow at me with a silent question. She knows why I left all those years ago.

My shoulders lift and fall nonchalantly but I can't fight shooting a wink which makes her laugh. After a few minutes of playing catch up and confirming that my return is permanent she stares at me, her gaze bores into my soul and she lets out an excited gasp.

"You've got a lady friend! Did you bring her back with you? How did you meet?" She rapid-fires question after question before I hold up my hands in surrender and explain as much as I can. Nina's story is her own to share after all.

Twenty minutes later I've got a bouquet of sunflowers and pink roses in hand with a promise that it will have Nina devoting herself to me. My mind begins to wonder at the possibilities after that comment as I return to the car and stare out the window watching the town pass by while we head back to my house. My phone dings with a notification dragging my attention away from my completely inappropriate thoughts.

Mother:

> Where the hell are you! Milo has everyone here, Jade has everything ready, and Abel just messaged saying that they'll be here in twenty minutes!

I shake my head and put my phone away as we pull into the driveway, the front door swings open as soon as I step out. My feet move forward with purpose as I approach, the scowl on my mother's face has me chuckling.

"I was talking to Aunt C, I haven't seen her since I've been home. It's not like I would let Nina beat me home." I roll my eyes at her, "You know I had Abel messaging me when I was at the thirty-minute mark."

She swats my chest in the same way Celeste did not long ago, I groan in annoyance since my mother didn't hold back. I step aside and walk toward the kitchen where my men who have been a constant in Nina's life since she's arrived here, Aunt Tabs and Jade are waiting for us. I turn and grin at my mother who is hot on my heels and pull her into a hug.

"Thank you for doing this for her." I praise my mom who pushes me away so she can join Milo and Jade by the counter. My eye twitches at the sight of them being so goddamn obvious. They're not even attempting to hide it anymore. I can't wait to end this shit with Barone so I can kill my best friend.

A few minutes later, Nina and Brittany walk into the kitchen carrying several black bags along with an obviously amused Abel, and stoned face Rand.

"Happy birthday, Short Stack." I grin at her as I step forward and pull her into my arms, my mouth crashes against hers as I take the kiss I've needed since I left her this morning. It only lasts a moment before we separate.

"Hi," her breathy response has my dick hardening in my pants. Nina glances around and her cheeks flush as she takes in everyone who is here. "What's going on?"

Brittany snorts from behind us and quietly says "Surprise, Tink. It's your birthday party."

Nina's eyes go wide as she looks at me and down at her hands before glancing back up at me. I cock a brow at her, but don't say anything as I hand her the flowers. She instinctively reaches out to take them from me but loses grip on her bags, which drop to the ground. An audible buzz sounds from the bags which makes Abel burst out in laughter, while Nina's face pales to a sickly white. Her eyes don't leave mine as Brittany kneels down to pick them up. She fails horribly at hiding her laughter, even more so when something bright pink rolls out. I glance down at the ground, my own grin unable to be contained at this point. Nina's chest and cheeks could rival Ariel's hair color. I take a step toward her to try to ease the discomfort until I hear a voice behind me speak up.

"That thing will blow your mind!" Milo's remark is met with an audible slap followed immediately by my mother's voice.

"*Idiota!*"

My expression must show the rage that the exchange between my mother and Milo solidified for me on what I already assumed was happening because Nina lunges forward and wraps her arms around me. Her body trembles against me as I encase my arms around her, finding solace in her embrace.

"I'm so sorry," she whispers into my neck as tears coat my neck. "I won't use them."

When the meaning behind her words registers, I lift her into my arms and carry her across the open space of the kitchen toward the pantry. My hand presses against the frosted glass door and it swings against the wall just enough to rattle whatever is on the shelves before I slap it closed. I set her down and lean down so my face is mere inches from hers.

"*Amore mio*, I want you to understand something right now. I would never be upset with you over something like this." I cup her cheeks between my palms and press my mouth to hers briefly, separating just long enough to make sure I'm crystal fucking clear. "If you want to use toys with me, without me, on me. I will do any fucking thing that will make you happy and bring you pleasure."

Her eyes blink rapidly as I speak, her breaths are still coming out in quick succession.

"*Bella*, the anger you saw out there wasn't even close to being directed toward you." A gentle smile pulls at the corners of my mouth as she begins to calm down. "Why don't you head back to our room. I'll meet you there in a few minutes, alright?"

 Chapter 30
Johnny

Once the door is closed behind me, I turn the lock before I step further into our space. Nina's sitting on the bed, her face in her hands, her bare legs on full display with the flared mini skirt she has on. My eyes roam up her body realizing she's wearing another low-cut crop top. A sly grin twists my lips, my girl isn't afraid to show off some skin.

I cautiously drop the bag on the ground and kick off my shoes leaving them by the door before I approach her. She glances up at me as soon as she senses the movement. Her expression softens when she realizes I'm alone. I take a seat next to her, my arm tugging her into my side.

"*Bella*, may I ask you a question?" I break the silence; the curiosity burns through my veins. She lifts her gaze to meet mine as she waits for me to continue. "Why did you decide to buy all of that today?"

She blanches and tries to pull away, but I hold her tight against my side, not allowing her to hide. After a long huff she replies.

"Brittany said that I needed to practice before we went any further." She groans and drops her face back into her hands.

My shoulders shake with laughter which pisses her off. She smacks my chest. God damnit! What is it with women and my damn chest today? I lower myself to the floor to kneel in front of her. I drag her hands from her face and cup her cheeks so she can't look away from me.

"You don't need toys to practice, and I'm honored that you want to go further." My lips pull into a sinful smirk at the ideas that are bouncing around my head. "Tell me what it is you want, and I'll make it happen."

Her eyes implore me silently, I don't move or speak, needing to hear the words. Until I know what she's ready for, I'm not going to go balls to the wall. Even if I'd willingly throw myself in front of a rocket launcher to be with her. I need her enthusiastic consent, especially given her lack of experience.

"I want you." Her words are a soft whisper, the confident woman that has been peeking through recently, nowhere to be seen. She must see that I'm not willing to budge for her on this. "I'm a twenty-five-year-old virgin, Giovanni. I want you to fuck me, I'm tired of not knowing what it's like to be with someone so completely that nothing else matters. I know there is something between us and dammit – I don't want to wait. Please." Her confidence is returning or at least an illusion of confidence.

"You're sure?" I hate myself for asking the question, but I wouldn't feel right without confirmation.

"Yes." That one word has my cock standing at full attention.

Without another word, I stand to my full height, her eyes trail my every move as she sits up straight. I shrug out of my suit jacket and toss it on the ground behind me, not giving a single fuck about how much the dry cleaner is going to be pissed at my lack of respect for fashion. Nina's breath catches as my mouth finds hers for a quick kiss.

"Before anything else happens, I'm going to undress you. Ok?" I keep my eyes on hers as I wait for a response. Her lips turn up at the corner as she nods. My heart beats chaotically in my chest like a racquetball being shot from a ball launcher as I reach forward and begin my task. I lift her shirt, pulling it up over her head to find she's bare underneath which pulls a groan from deep within my chest. "*Bella.*"

The sweetest giggle passes her lips as I take in her bare breasts, her nipples pebbled and begging for my attention. It's not the first time, but knowing that there will be more happening tonight has my cock leaking like a teenager just at the gorgeous sight before me. I dip my head and swirl my tongue around the tight peak, her back arches at the sensation. My fingers hook under the waistband of her skirt, she lifts her hips to allow me to drag them down her toned legs. My eyes land on the black lace thong she's wearing, the noticeable wet patch has me leaning in to smell her dampness.

I press my nose against Nina's panties and inhale deeply, the scent of her arousal making me feral for her. Unable to take my time any longer I grip the waistband of the thong, tearing it off her body. She lets out a gasp as she watches me drag the scrap of cloth down her leg tossing it somewhere out of sight. I press my mouth to her inner thigh and nip gently.

"Giovanni," my whispered name sounds like a prayer on her lips. "Can I undress you?"

My heart swells at her request. She's so fucking incredible and I'm going to make her mine in every fucking way I can as soon as she'll allow it.

"As you wish, *Bella.*"

Her delicate hands work methodically as she kneels on the bed in front of me. Fingers tremble as they unbutton my dress shirt. When I shrug the shirt off, she steps down from the bed and kneels in front of me.

"Seeing you on your knees for me is a beautiful fucking sight, Nina." The corners of her mouth turn up at the praise as she concentrates on removing my pants. She tugs at the waistband; her fingers hook under both my pants and boxers. She hasn't seen everything she's in for yet. I made sure of that when she asked me to stroke my cock in front of her, getting into a position that wouldn't scare her off right away.

As soon as my cock springs free her face falls with fear as she backs away. Quickly climbing onto the bed, she scrambles as far away as she can get from me. I chuckle at her reaction, not entirely surprised.

"That! That's supposed to go inside me?" Her question has me fighting back tears of laughter. "Did it grow? And where did all that come from?" She asks as she gestures toward the part of my dick she didn't see before, "There's no way that will fit!"

I kick off my pants and crawl up the bed to get closer to her. She pulls her legs into her chest, but I drag them back toward me as soon as I reach her.

"*Amore mio*, it's a Jacobs ladder piercing. It's not going to hurt you, if anything it's just going to intensify your pleasure. I just need to get you ready for me." I dip my head and press my lips against her ankle before trailing a few kisses up her calf. "Do you trust me?"

Nina's head shakes an exasperated "no" until I grip her ankles and pull her toward me, her body stays rigid, but she doesn't fight me or ask me to stop. I lift her other ankle to my mouth trailing soft kisses similarly to what I did a moment ago. However, this time I don't stop at her calf. My lips travel up until I land at the apex of her thighs. I bury my face between her legs and inhale deeply. The scent of her arousal is still strong. I know she wants this, my tongue darts out and slides between her folds swirling quickly around her swollen clit.

"Fuck!" She cries out as her hand grips my hair. My smile turns wicked against her pretty pussy as I grip her thighs and part her even more for me. A sinful idea enters my mind as soon as her entrance is within my line of sight. I swipe my tongue against her opening knowing this will be the first time anything has penetrated it. Soft whimpers from above have me pausing my task. "No! Don't stop, God, fuck. Yes, I trust you, please."

I chuckle against her and prod her entrance again; I can feel her walls quivering around me already, and it's fucking glorious. I remove my tongue from her cunt as I return my attention to her clit. Nina's sobs and pleas of pleasure are nearly incoherent as I drag my hand to her entrance and slide a finger inside her virgin hole. Her pussy clenches around me immediately at the intrusion.

"Relax, *Amore*, you know how good I've made you feel. I'm not going to do anything to make you uncomfortable." My words seem to offer the reaffirmation that she needs because a long breath passes her lips as she melts into the mattress. "That's my good girl. You're doing so well, *Bella.*"

I dip my head down, my mouth latches around her clit as I suck the sensitive bundle of nerves into my mouth. My name comes out as a chant as I find her G-spot with the finger that is inside her. I press firmly as I massage her inner channel while my mouth continues to suck in a torturous rhythm.

"Mmm ooo mmm fuuuuc," Nina's release is imminent based on how she bucks up, fucking my finger, and forcing more friction against her clit. The strangulation of my fingers from her release causes my appendages to begin to lose feeling. My eyes trail up her body to see her face as she detonates around me. Fuck, she's perfect. I lap up her release, which elicits the most incredible sounds from her parted lips just before I crawl up her body and press my lips to hers, allowing her to taste herself on my lips.

By the time I've given her one more orgasm with my mouth, Nina's body is pliant enough to fully claim her. I reach over where she lays under me toward the bedside table I had stocked with a box of condoms. When I reach for the pack, I groan when I pull it out and see that it's open with only one left. I can't think about who took them right now. I should be thankful that they're being safe. Gross, no. I can't think about that right now.

"*Amore*, it seems as though someone has helped themselves to the stash of condoms I put in here. We only have one." I explain as I tear open the foil wrapper with my teeth. She nods in response as I sheath my cock, making a show out of it for her. The way her body is trembling with need under me has my dick ready to fucking explode. There's no way I'll be able to last.

With her thighs spread I loom over her and press my lips against her mouth one more time before I align myself with her entrance and press the thick head just past her opening.

"Oh, God!" Passes her lips as a plea.

"You're doing so well, *Amore*," I praise as I glide my thumb over her clit before I slightly pull out so I can inch back in. Her walls constrict as my hand expertly massages the overly sensitive bundle of nerves. A symphony of sounds of the pleasure I'm giving her has my controlled movements becoming more difficult the deeper I get. Nina's body was fucking made for me, and I haven't even broken through yet. Fuck. I'm only a few inches in when I feel it, the proof of her innocence. "*Amore Mio*, this next part isn't going to feel great, but I promise you, I will make it feel good once we're through. Are you ok if I keep going?"

"If you think stopping is an option, you've lost your fucking mind. I don't care if it hurts. I need you." She urges me deeper and lifts her hips before I can stop her. The movement has me losing my balance and I bottom out inside her glorious cunt. My body goes still when she sobs in pain. Her chest heaves as the reality of what just happened overwhelms her.

I press my lips to her neck as her body trembles underneath me. I begin to massage her clit between us again which helps her relax back into what we're doing. Nina's pelvis begins to rock with the motion of my thumb as her arms wrap around my back, her nails dig into my skin as she urges me on. She's so fucking tight, her walls begin to convulse around me. I groan as I rut my hips into her.

"*Bella*, I'm not going to last, I need you to come with me, *Amore Mio*." I force out through gritted teeth as I try to hold back. She screams out a second later as her cunt squeezes my cock, strangling my length. I can feel the piercings dragging against her tight channel more than I'm used to, and the sensation's sends me over the edge.

"Gio –" my name is cut off as I thrust inside her harder than I had, the movement taking her by surprise before I still, emptying myself into the condom.

"Nina!" Her name comes out in a guttural moan as my vision goes fuzzy. "Fuck!"

I collapse on top of her, our chests heaving against one another as we catch our breaths. When my brain restarts after the incredible fucking release, I prop myself up onto my elbows to stare into her eyes. I realize there are tears streaming down her cheeks. My instinct is to pull out quickly and apologize but the expression on her face isn't one of regret or hurt, it's one of an all-consuming peace.

"Hey," I gently press my mouth against her bruised lips. "What do you need?" I ask as my cock pulses inside her and she moans into the kiss.

"More of that, every day for the rest of my life." She admits, her cheeks flush as she fights a grin.

Chapter 31

A familiar voice calls my name pulling me from my slumber. I groan as reality begins to fade into the forefront of my consciousness. Pleasure and pain radiate through my entire body with every stretch I take as the memories of last night replay in my mind. My muscles are so deliciously sore. I feel like a new woman, in a way I suppose I am. When my eyelids flutter open, I catch sight of Giovanni fully dressed in one of his beautifully custom-tailored suits. Incoherent sounds pass my lips as I try to pull him back into bed with me. A deep chuckle reverberates through his chest as he looms over me.

"Good morning, *Amore Mio*." He whispers the greeting just before his mouth gently presses to mine for the briefest of kisses. "I'm sorry to wake you, *Bella*. I just didn't want you to wake up and me not be here without an explanation. I have some –" his words die on this tongue briefly. I can practically see the wheels turn in his head as he contemplates just how much he is going to tell me before he makes a decision to be truthful. "I have a few more people to question in order to find out how deep things are with your father before we take him out."

A blissful sigh escapes my lips as he drones on about my father. Is it sad that I don't care what happens to the man that provided half of my DNA anymore? Not that he ever cared about me, that much has become clearer than an invisible dog fence over the time I've been free and with the Ludovico family.

"As long as you come home to me, do what you need to." I sigh, full of contentment. "Although, I don't know that I'll be doing much moving today anyway. After that last position, I'm pretty sure any flexibility I possessed has now vanished." My skin heats when I realize what I've said aloud. Giovanni chuckles darkly, the gleam in his eyes tells me he's thinking of every dirty thing he did to me last night.

His lips ghost against mine before he pulls away and stands to his full height. I prop myself up onto my elbow as I pull the blanket snug around my bare chest. Not that anything was showing before. His wicked smirk melts my insides as he retreats toward the door. Before he closes it behind him, he calls across the room to me.

"Rest up, *Amore Mio*. I have so much more planned for you tonight." The sensual tone of his voice bathes me in anticipation. I feel my skin prick as goosebumps cover my entire body.

Once I'm alone with my own thoughts my brain is on full steam ahead, unable to stop thinking about what more there could be for him to do to me. Don't get me wrong, I'm ready, willing, and able. The curiosity is going to have me on edge all day. With the realization that I won't be able to fall back to sleep, I throw off the blankets and sit up to stretch my muscles. The cool breeze from the ceiling fan sends a chill through my still naked body. I scramble to the bathroom ready to warm up in the shower while I reluctantly wash off the evidence of last night's events.

I step through the doorway of the kitchen to find Vanna sitting at the island as usual, but she's on her laptop today. Jade is bouncing around like the ridiculously productive woman I've come to know and love. My lips curve up into a grin as it dawns on me that I love this family. I try to walk as discreetly as possible toward them.

Jade glances in my direction for a second with a knowing smirk before she goes back to her task. Meanwhile Vanna's gaze lands on me and she arches a brow. As I slide into the seat next to her she wraps her arm around my shoulder and chuckles.

"Well, it looks like he finally staked his claim. Are you ok?" Her sweet maternal instinct to care for me makes me feel lighter. I do need to talk because so much has happened in the last twelve hours alone.

A breath whooshes from my body as I exhale deeply before I proceed with the events that lead to this morning.

"Yes, we had sex. It was amazing and terrifying. He's so big and he's got piercings. Is that normal? How many times in one night is normal? Is it normal that I'm so sore?" I rapid fire my questions at her one by one. Jade chokes on the coffee she's sipping as Vanna stares at me with her mouth agape. My gaze darts back and forth between the two women with confusion when I'm met with silence. "What? Did I do something wrong?"

"Jesus, what is with these boys and piercings?" Vanna mumbles under her breath. "Sweetheart, I love you like you're my blood, but this is just not a conversation I can have about my son. Let's call Brittany and get her over here so you can talk everything out. Ok?" She offers as she pulls me in for a tighter hug as she picks up her phone and quickly taps on the screen. Presumably to send a message to Brittany.

My skin heats as I realize that my instinct to share everything with them isn't the best idea in this situation. Vanna must notice my embarrassment because she places the device back on the counter and turns to face me. Her hands cup my cheeks and she offers me the sweetest and warmest smile as I shrink into myself.

"Hey, don't do that. You didn't do anything wrong. You didn't know. If it were anyone else, I'd have the conversation with you, but as a mother, the last thing I want or need to know about is my child's sex life. I was only eighteen when I had him and sometimes it's hard to believe he's grown enough to be having sex." She shakes her head with a slight smile as she appears lost in a memory. "He was my little Leo through and through, between his generosity and his need to protect those he cares about. You're in good hands, Nina."

A strong vibration tickles my butt-cheek as a text message comes through my phone I forgot in my back pocket. I giggle to myself as I pull the device out to find a message from Giovanni.

Giovanni:

> How are you feeling?

My lips curve up into a bigger grin as I quickly type back a response.

Nina:

> Sore, but good. Ready to find out what you have in store for me tonight.

Giovanni:

> You'll have to wait a little longer, don't worry we'll still have plenty of time for me to demonstrate exactly what I have in mind when we get home. I'm taking you to dinner first. Be ready to leave by seven.

His response is immediate and the words have me clenching my thighs together. How is it that such simple words can have me on the edge of my seat with excitement and need.

I groan quietly to myself before I shove my phone back into the pocket of my jeans. A moment later Vanna walks toward me with Brittany trailing behind her with the widest smile.

"Tink! How dare you!" She squeals as she rushes up to me and pulls me in for a hug.

"Huh?" My eyes fly around the room as she spins us in a circle until they land on Vanna who has a mischievous smirk on her face. "How dare I what?" Her choice of wording has my body stiff as a board until I force myself to take a few breaths and remember where I am, who I'm with.

"I had to hear from Vanna that you lost your V-card! Seriously, I thought we were friends!" She shouts excitedly.

My shoulders shake with uncontrollable laughter. The last time someone approached me like that was my father because I stood by the window too long when he had people over that could have seen me. He beat me so badly I couldn't get out of bed for two days that time. Now, I'm being scolded for not getting in touch with my friend immediately after losing my virginity. I shake my head and hug Brittany tight before I drag her behind me to lay everything out on the table.

The rest of the day goes by so fast I lose track of time. It's not until Michael walks into the living room where Brittany and I are still talking that I'm reminded I need to get ready. The man towers in the doorway as he clears his throat before entering.

"Sorry to bother you, Johnny sent me back early to pick you up. He's running a bit behind and will need to meet you at the restaurant. Since Abel has the day off, I'll be driving you." He offers a kind smile before turning away.

Brittany jumps to her feet and scrambles around the giant man. He dwarfs her with his giant frame, so much so that I can't even see her from my position on the couch, and I have to cover my mouth to stifle the giggle.

"Hey, Daddy." I hear her muffled voice from wherever she stands in front of him. "When are you going to let me take you for a ride?"

Chapter 32

Nina

When I step out of the bathroom dressed and ready to go, Brittany's eyes go wide as soon as she sees me. Suddenly feeling self-conscious, I glance down over my choice of dress. The last message I received from Giovanni said cocktail attire. I thought this would be ok. My heart thuds hard in my chest as I use my arms as a shield, covering as much of myself as I can.

"Don't you dare! You are fucking hot as hell. Spin for me!" My cheeks heat but I do as she asks. Her eyes light up when I'm facing her again.

"How the hell did you even get that zipped all the way?" She asks motioning at the full-length zipper on the back of the dress. I laugh at the memory as I explain zipping it in front and turning it around so that I could put my arms in the sleeves. It's a curve hugging long sleeve cocktail dress I found in Tab's collection.

"I figured since we're nearing the end of October it would be best to wear something that covered at least a little bit of skin." My lips curve as I pull the strap of the heel around my ankle before doing the same to the other side. "I really look ok?"

"You're going to be lucky if that man makes it through dinner before he fucks you. God damn woman." She laughs at her crassness which only amuses me more.

Michael's eyes sparkle with pride when he sees me as I carefully cross the driveway to the car, still not used to heels, but the more I wear them, the easier they are to wear. My hands wrap around the beaded clutch that Tabs insisted on when I bought this dress as I approach the vehicle. His hand grips the door handle as he pulls it open so I can enter.

"You look beautiful. I know it hasn't been long since we were introduced, but I'm so proud of you. We all are, you've come so far already. I can't wait to see you shine, Nina." Michael holds out his hand to help me slide into the car.

"Thank you, that means a lot." I lift my gaze to meet his before I slide into my seat.

Our drive to the restaurant is quick. I'm staring out the driver's side rear window lost in a day dream when the door next to me opens. My heart drops into my stomach as I let out a surprised gasp. When I look up to see Giovanni caging me in the car, I grin up at him as his eyes roam up and down my body.

"Are you going to help me out or are you going to stare all night?" My eyes gleam with mischief. He really is going to lose his mind when he gets a glimpse of the back of my dress.

Giovanni clears his throat and holds his hand out helping me to my feet. The building in front of us is hidden by so many trees, the windows are covered in ivy with the most beautiful pink flowers blooming along the walls. *What is this place,* I wonder as we approach a large white sign with beautiful black cursive lettering that answers my question. *C'est La Vie.* With his hand on the small of my back, he guides me across the sidewalk through the entrance of what appears to be a French restaurant.

As soon as we reach the hostess, she greets Giovanni like they're old friends and leads us to a table toward the back of the restaurant. When he gestures for me to walk ahead of him, I fight to stifle the giggle and add a little bounce to my step. I'm feeling so confident with this dress, it may become dangerous. My eyes dart around the room as I take in the limited number of people dining here tonight. When I take my seat and face him, the beautiful insightful man I've come to know so well answers before I can ask.

"I paid for half of the restaurant so you wouldn't have to deal with as much of a crowd." His eyes crease at the corners as he smiles warmly at me while he helps me move my chair under the table. I was so overwhelmed by the building I didn't realize he's in a blue suit that matches my dress. Down to the silver - grey tie that matches my zipper. "You look stunning, and that dress is doing things to me that you will pay for later, Short Stack." He winks before pressing a quick kiss to my red painted lips. My body melts into my chair as his words and that chaste kiss bathe me in anticipation. I inwardly groan knowing he's going to make the rest of the evening torturous.

Giovanni takes his place at the table across from me and motions for a server to come over. The man doesn't speak, but fills fancy tall glasses with a fizzy liquid I've never seen before. My expression must show my confusion.

"It's champagne, to hopefully celebrate –" he begins as he lifts my glass and hands it to me before taking his own. His glass gently clinks against mine before he takes a sip and I do the same, the feel of bubbles popping against my nose makes me jump just as the liquid reaches my tongue. My face contorts as I swallow the awful liquid, "Ok, so you're not a champagne person, we'll figure that out later when less is going on." He chuckles as I glare at him.

"Why do people drink this?" I ask, lowering the glass back to the table as I exchange it for a glass of water. His broad shoulders shake with laughter as he takes another sip of the awful drink.

The server returns not long after and takes our order. I'm not exactly sure what is ordered because the menu is in French. I'm assured I'll like it, but raise a questioning brow at the man across from me considering what he just tricked me into drinking. He smiles and holds out his hand across the table for me to take, which of course I do.

"I have a reason for wanting to take you out tonight." His lips twist into a sinful grin. "Last night was..." His words die as he stares at me as if he's reliving the events right now. My cheeks flush under his sinful gaze as he continues, "incredible. I haven't stopped thinking all day about how good you feel around me. I've been hard as stone since I had to leave you this morning."

His gaze rakes across my chest as I take in deep breaths while he continues, confused by where this is going.

"I wanted to see how you were doing without any curious ears lurking around corners." He smirks, "While the men work for me, if any of them thought that I hurt you or upset you, they'd take me out in an instant. You've got every single one of them smitten with you, *Amore Mio*." His fingers wrap around mine as he holds my trembling hand in his. "Hell, I'm so far gone for you, I'll leave a trail of bodies behind if anyone so much as takes a breath in your vicinity."

Before I can form a response, a throat clears to the right of me. When I glance up to find my father's face, my body recoils. Fear, anger, anxiety, and pain are just a few of the emotions that the man's presence elicits.

"Nina, It's nice to see you. Can we chat?" His gaze trails to Giovanni who is glaring daggers, "In private."

My body is incapable of moving even if I wanted to, when I sense the rage boiling under his skin, I turn to my father. And for the first time, I'm not worried about repercussions of not giving in to what he wants.

"No, anything you'd like to say to me you can say in front of Giovanni. He knows everything. Every. Thing." My hatred for my own flesh and blood is something I never expected, but as I've learned the truth after the time with the only family that has ever actually treated me as such, I'm done. Done just rolling over and doing what I'm told. I'm not his prisoner any longer.

"You stupid little," He begins to raise his hand to hit me. Before the appendage reaches halfway up his torso, Giovanni stands and takes hold of my father. I can't see my father's face any longer, for which I'm grateful. However, the words that come out of the man I care so deeply for send a chill of excitement through me.

"If you speak to or treat her with any kind of disrespect again, I will slit your throat and feed you your own windpipe before your body even has a chance to reach the ground. Do you understand me, you slimy mother fucker?"

My father's intense glare is locked on Giovanni when he speaks again.

"This isn't over. I'll see you soon, kid." Before he disappears from our table, he makes it a point to drag his hand through his hair in a way that he used to taunt me with. I was never sure if he was going to hit me when he did this. However, for the first time in years, I don't flinch at the action.

Chapter 33

The rest of our dinner went as smoothly as can be expected after my father left. Giovanni hasn't allowed a moment to pass since we were at the restaurant that some part of him hasn't been touching me. I've been relishing in the constant contact, it's allowed a peace to take over instead of the other emotions that my father brings out of me. Our car pulls up just outside of the front door. I feel his eyes boring into the side of my cheek as I stare out the window. He reluctantly releases his hold on me as he slides out into the dark night. I'm lost in my own thoughts, unsure of the feelings that have come to the surface tonight.

I startle when my door opens his concerned expression makes me realize my silence as I process how this has been affecting him. When he reaches out to help me out, I leap out of the car and wrap my arms around his middle. A whoosh of air rushes past his lips as he wraps himself around me, and lets out the anxiety I inadvertently caused.

"*Bella*, none of this is your fault." He whispers into my ear as he holds me tight. I lift my chin to look up into his beautiful brown eyes and offer a reassuring smile. My hold around him loosens enough to grab his hand and lead him inside to our room.

When we're finally in the safety of our sanctuary, he closes the door behind him, the click of the lock makes me smile. I hear the thud of his shoes hit the floor as he kicks them off mere seconds before I feel him at my back. His solid wall of warm muscle molds to me perfectly.

"*Amore Mio*, are you ok?" Giovanni's lips are at my ear as he whispers his question. "I didn't expect him to show up like that."

My shoulders sag when he brings up my father. I spin in his arms to face him, my hands reach for him and cup his face. Our eyes lock on one another for several moments before I step up onto my tiptoes and pull his face to meet mine. Our lips press firmly together for several beats before I pull away.

"I want to forget about him. Tonight was supposed to be for us, help me forget." I stare into the depth of his beautiful chocolate gaze. A sinful and mischievous glint lights his eyes as he peels his suit jacket off and tosses it on the chair behind him. He steps into my space, forcing me to move backward as he loosens the silver tie around his neck. He lifts it over his head and tosses it somewhere behind him, forgotten the moment it's out of sight.

The moment he begins to untuck his button up, my mouth goes dry. With every single button that is undone, my body is forced backwards until my thighs hit the bed. My throat bobs as I swallow hard when he shrugs off the shirt, his bare chest on full display. His chest is covered in breathtaking art, no matter how many times I see it, my heart stutters. Giovanni's hands land on my hips as he spins me to face the bed. A squeal escapes at the sudden change in position.

Giovanni gathers my hair in his hand as he piles the wild mane on my left shoulder. I feel his breath grow closer as he dips his head to press soft kisses against my neck. The sensation sends a jolt of heat directly to my core. I feel him smile against the same spot when he lifts his hands to the zipper of my dress.

"*Bella*, this dress has had my cock leaking since you stepped out of that car." His smooth voice bathes me in anticipation while he slides his fingers under the fabric to slide it off my body. "I am going to bury myself so deep inside you, there's no telling where I end and you begin." He slaps my ass to punctuate his point, a feral growl sounds from deep in his chest when the impact reverberates against my skin. He steps away and turns me back to face him. I can see the heat fill his gaze the moment his eyes land at the apex of my thighs. Excitement and a bit of the possessiveness I love to see on him when he realizes that I haven't had anything on under the dress at all. "Oh, *Amore Mio.*"

He guides me to lower myself on the bed. My lips curl up into a sinful smile as I take in the beautiful man before me. Before I can make a comment on how much I need him. He's already propped on his elbows between my legs. His face dips out of sight and I feel his breath against my sensitive flesh.

I cry out with pleasure when his tongue swirls sweet circles around my clit. I've lost count of just how many orgasms I've had this way. My thighs tremble as they clamp hard against his ears when my release rolls through my body once again. My chest heaves with heavy breaths when he finally lets up. I whimper as a slight breeze rushes over my pussy. Everything is so much more sensitive, I feel like I could scream.

My eyes go wide when I try to prop myself up on my elbows, hands grip my ankles and I'm flipped onto my stomach. No longer able to see the man who continues to worship my body, I begin to ache for his expertise again. You'd think I haven't been forced to climax multiple times since we got home with how badly I need to come again.

"Lift your ass up for me, *Bella.*" His sultry voice taunts me.

I immediately follow his instruction like the good girl I want to be for him when the sting of another smack lands. My lips part with a needy gasp. I feel him between my legs and press myself backward to feel him, the action only results in another stinging slap against my tender cheek.

"So greedy, *Amore.*" The grin on his face is obvious with his tone. Without another word, I feel the thick tip of his cock nudge against my entrance. I let out a sigh of relief when he presses himself inside. The more of him I get, the more of him I need. Giovanni slowly begins to pump his hips in and out of my tight pussy, my body becomes impatient and I force myself backward, sheathing him to the hilt. A delicious groan sounds as he exclaims, "Jesus Christ."

When I match his every thrust, his fingers dig into my hips as he tries to slow me down. A pulsing sensation inside me has me crying out with desire. I feel him grow harder inside me with every pump of his hips. My lips curve up at the corners knowing that the more my confidence grows inside the bedroom the more aroused he becomes, which I didn't realize was possible. Sudden emptiness makes my head spin as he flips me onto my back and slides back home.

Dark brown eyes roam my body as he lifts my legs over his shoulders. My mouth parts as incoherent sounds leave my body with every way he positions me, only to make the pleasure more intense. When I feel his arm wrap around the outside of my thigh to hold me in place, while his other expertly teases my clit, my body vibrates with anticipation.

A breath is lodged in my lungs when the overwhelming stimulation of being filled with his cock and worked over with his fingers like a goddamn guitar string have me shooting over the edge. My screams of pleasure come out silently when I forget to breathe until Giovanni pinches my clit between his thumb and forefinger, causing an explosion of rolling orgasms. His eyes sparkle with pleasure when he stills inside me, the sensation of his cum filling me makes my pussy clench harder around him. Fuck, why does this feel so good?

"Fuck me, you just milked my soul from my dick." Giovanni grunts as he collapses on top of me and presses his lips to mine in a heated kiss. He presses his forehead to mine before he rolls off of me and onto his side a second later, strong arms pull me back into his chest as he dozes off.

My mind hasn't calmed down even after several mind-blowing and explosive orgasms. The anger I feel over the threat my father attempted to impose tonight is too much. My hair is still damp from the shower I took before coming to the gym, but I don't give a damn if I drip on the mats. When I open the door to find Michael using the punching bag I smile, even if I want to punch him since I have to wait.

"Couldn't sleep?" He smiles knowingly at me.

I shrug my shoulders as I pad over to the dreaded treadmill. My cheeks heat when I feel his gaze locked on me.

"Get over here. I'll spar with you, kid." His kind offer is met with a wide grin on my end.

Nothing feels quite as good as beating your frustration and anger out against someone who is easily three times your size. Michael is a good-looking guy, even if he's closer to my dad's age. I can see why Brittany is drawn to him the way she is.

The past twenty minutes of dancing around him, blocking his shots, and throwing punches of my own has my blood pumping. I feel a sense of pride fill me each time I get to practice with him. When we started, he told me his goal is for me to be able to take Giovanni down. My goal is to be able to take Michael down. One day it will happen, and I know that the ability to lay him out on his ass means that my father will never be able to hurt me again. My closed fist lands hard against his jaw, sending him stumbling backwards. I scream, worried I've hurt the giant, and rush toward him.

"Oh my God, are you ok?" I shriek out.

Michael's chuckle sends a rush of relief through me. When his eyes meet mine, his grin is wider than I've ever seen.

"You're doing good, kid." His expression changes as he considers something. "Can I ask you something?" I've never seen a man appear to be sheepish before this moment.

"Sure, anything." My curiosity is killing me as I stand still and wait for him to proceed.

"What's Brittany's deal?"

"Deal? What do you mean?" My brow furrows as I try to understand his question. When I'm unable to comprehend what he's trying to ask, I attempt to get clarification, but Michael cuts me off.

"Never mind - it's a bad idea." He shrugs his shoulders and walks out of the gym without a glance back at me.

Chapter 34
Johnny

Michael and Milo have been out chasing down what we expect to be the last of the leads before I have enough to end all of this bullshit with Nina's father. We've spent the last six months tracking down anyone associated with the shit stain of a human that is Mateo Barone. In my life, there have been a total of three people I've hated. I had one killed in prison, and then I slit the throat of my grandfather. The moment I get to put a bullet between Mateo's eyes will be one of the best of my life. Granted, I don't see much of anything topping the moment my eyes landed on Nina.

Danny Boy's erratic driving has me on edge. We've been weaving in and out of traffic on the drive here. The moment he pulls into a spot in the underground parking garage, I breathe out a sigh of relief. I never thought I'd be happy to have a meeting with the mayor.

"Remind me never to get into a car that you're driving again after today. Jesus fucking Christ." My complaint is met with a snort when Danny steps out of the car and follows closely behind me.

The moment I step inside the modern building, my eyes are assaulted by so much white. The walls are painted with such an intense shade of white, I need sunglasses to process what the hell is in front of me.

"Would it be rude to offer the name of an interior designer the first time I meet this woman?" I mumble under my breath to Danny who tries and fails to stifle a laugh.

As we walk deeper into the space, I'm greeted by a familiar face that I haven't seen since graduating high school. Not much has changed about him over the years. He was never a bad looking dude, tall, buff, but damn, was the fucker a bully.

"Damn, Giovanni Ludovico. I never thought I'd see the day you'd be back in town." Peter Knight grins from behind a desk as he reaches out to shake my hand. A twisted glint in his eye is evident as he proceeds. "Last I heard, you left when you caught your woman banging gramps. Sorry about that."

My gaze lands on his outstretched hand and raises back to the face of a man who just insulted me. I imagine every way I could possibly remove the appendage from his body. From the most to least painful. Bloodiest to cleanest, the possibilities are endless.

"How about we don't play like we were friends." My lips pull up into a wide sinister grin as I lean in to speak into his ear. "You were the biggest dick in high school, and if I had been the one to catch you doing even a fraction of the shit you got in trouble with, my career would have begun much sooner."

The man isn't a total idiot because he returns to his seat. He lifts the receiver to his desk phone to his ear and presses a few buttons on the display. After a moment, he speaks softly into the handset and places it back down. When he lifts his gaze to meet mine, he smirks at me.

"Mayor Ricci will be with you momentarily. Please have a seat." The asshole gestures toward a handful of dark leather chairs in a designated waiting area across from him.

The universe seems to be on my side today, because the office door opens and a woman dressed in a black suit steps out. She's a nice-looking woman, close to my age, maybe a little older, with sandy colored hair and light blue eyes. If I didn't suspect something happening with Brittany and Michael, I would suggest he get in touch with her. She looks like the type of woman he's generally been caught up with.

"Mr. Ludocvico, it's a pleasure to meet you. I'm Mayor Taylor Ricci." Her genuine smile has me on edge. She's new to the position, so I have no idea what to expect in this conversation. "Please, join me in my office."

She gestures toward the door she stepped out of and begins to walk back toward the open door.

My feet move with purpose as I follow closely behind her. Once we're inside, she points to the chair in front of her desk before closing the door behind us. I sit back and cross my leg over my knee as I attempt to make myself comfortable on the hard, wooden chairs. The furniture in here doesn't seem like this woman. She's too sophisticated for this old-time ornate shit.

"Sorry about the furniture, I haven't had a chance to replace anything since I was sworn in last month. There seems to be bodies dropping every few days, which is taking my attention." She deadpans, her eyes locked on me. Mayor Ricci is trying to get me to admit to something.

"I've heard about that, I do hope you find out who is behind all of this soon." I offer a heartfelt smile.

She cocks a brow at me and laughs. "Cut the shit. I know who your family is Giovanni. My family was one that your charitable donations for legal aid allowed to get into Port Windsor legally." Mayor Ricci's solemn smile piques my curiosity, "My grandparents were trying to escape – well they never really went into detail with me. Even after my parents passed away and I lived with them, I didn't get the full story. However, they told me if your family ever showed up on my doorstep, I was to do whatever you wanted."

My chest fills with pride at her recollection of events. That is what our family was supposed to be about. Helping others make a life for themselves. Not helping them kill themselves.

"If I didn't know that the people you were dropping around the city were involved in the drug ring that popped up a few years ago, this would be a different conversation." The mayor explains.

"My family never condoned this type of shit in our town. I'm still trying to piece together what happened, but we're working to get the last of them out." I admit, "I will do my best to clean up the mess that was made, so long as you keep the police off my ass while I still have work to do."

Laughter echoes around the room as Mayor Ricci doubles over in a fit of giggles. I stand to check on her, but she waves me away. It takes a few moments before the woman is able to speak. Her eyes crinkle in the corner as she smiles up at me.

"If it means you rid this town of corrupt assholes, I'll make sure anything you do is piled onto the person behind the drug ring." She shrugs. "Does that make me corrupt? Maybe. But if it's going to keep my town safe, it's worth the risk." She admits with a wink.

The crazy woman is still laughing at herself as I stand to leave her office. My hand is wrapped around the door knob when I turn to face her again.

"Excuse me, Mayor." She glances up at me with an amused grin on her face. "I'll be in touch, but do me a favor. Keep an eye on Peter, he was a big problem in school and from what I can tell, things haven't changed much."

Danny Boy and I match each other's quick pace as we walk through the building back to the parking garage. I groan when I remember just how awful he drove before. My eyes land on him, and I silently hold my open hand out for the keys.

"No way! I'll behave. I love this car, Milo never lets me drive it. Please!" His plea amuses me and saying no isn't an option, so I shake my head with a laugh and let myself into the back seat. The kid is giddy when he gets behind the seat and starts the engine.

I pull my phone from my jacket pocket and press my contact for Michael. After a few rings, the line connects and I hear Milo in the background before Michael can even say hello. I spend the next few minutes explaining what was discussed between the Mayor and I. As I open my mouth to expand, my body is riddled with pain as a sudden impact jolts me forward.

Shots ring out, just as I feel something wet splatter onto my face and my vision goes dark.

Chapter 35

"I can't believe just how far you've come in such a short amount of time." Abel announces as he opens the door to the back of the SUV. While I've become used to being chauffeured around, I look forward to the day I can come here without bodyguards. Although, given Giovanni's lifestyle, it's unlikely to happen.

My lips twist into a genuine smile as I take in the man who has become so much like what I would assume is a big brother. He offers me a hand to help me out of the car. It feels like a long time, but in reality, I've only been with the Ludovico family for six months, maybe a little less. So much has happened, and yet, some days it feels like my life has still just begun.

Rand steps in front of Abel and me as he leads us into the coffee shop. The delicious scent of freshly roasted coffee beans makes my mouth water while we wait in line. I've only started to drink coffee after Giovanni insisted on waking me up with either his face or dick between my thighs every morning. It's been the only way I can get through the day. Granted, the man dicks me down so good that I'm not complaining. However, if I'm coming to hang out with Brittany while she's working, it's been requested that the guys bring me here to get us all caffeine.

The space that surrounds me is so fun, it makes me wish I felt comfortable enough to spend time here. Unfortunately, for my own lack of sanity, there is usually a crowd. I'm not quite ready for that yet. The large wall covered by fake ivy and greenery brightens up the grey brick walls around the rest of the space. Sleek wooden dining tables and chairs fill up most of the space, but my favorite thing about the design of this shop is the center; there are two huge, oversized leather couches facing one another. Four short stools cage in two coffee tables which are sandwiched between the couches. All of that, plus they roast their own beans on the premises, which is just an added bonus.

Abel nudges me with his shoulder as the man behind the counter motions for us. My cheeks heat when I realize I was daydreaming and not paying any attention to my surroundings. Oops.

It's been a tad on the slow side today, so Brittany and I have been having debates over the books she's introduced me to since we've met.

"Wait a minute here, you think that he is better than Wolf?" I stare at my friend with my jaw on the ground. I have a love for the book she introduced me to by Tess Watters, that her declaration that anyone could hold a candle to that man makes me clutch my imaginary pearls.

"Wait, what about the guy that named a restaurant after the eyeball lady?" An unexpected voice chimes in from behind us.

Brittany and I stop what we're doing and turn to face Rand whose cheeks are the rosiest I've ever seen. We exchange a look and burst into a fit of giggles.

"Rand! You read romance? Why didn't you tell us?" Brittany asks.

"You make me come in here nearly every day. You can't blame a guy for getting curious." The man who hardly speaks shrugs his shoulders and chuckles shyly. We're lost in the middle of a discussion on what Rand has read when the front door crashes open a few moments later.

My eyes go wide with fear and confusion when Michael and Milo rush in the store. No one speaks as they form a protective shield around Brittany and me while ushering us into separate cars. The drive back to the house seems to drag on forever, while my questions and pleas for answers are ignored. Frustration grows as my mind becomes a whirlwind of chaos and confusion unsure of what the hell could have caused this scenario.

When Brittany and I are reunited in the house, I cling to her. My heart beats like a snare drum in my chest with worry when I see the two women who have become sort of maternal figures to me rush to meet us in the foyer. I remove one of my hands from my friend to grab Vanna's hand. Abel runs off into the house on his own.

"What is going on? Where is Giovanni?" I beg once again for an answer which only becomes another plea ignored. After several moments and at Abel's return, we're ushered into the living room. It's impossible not to notice that every single window in the room has been covered by some security measure. I'm not sure what it is, but everything is blacked out. The only source of light is from the lamps illuminating the space.

Milo hasn't made eye contact with anyone since we've been home. Vanna must have noticed it too because she's the one that calls for him.

"Milo, look at me." This is the first time I've heard her confidence falter. "*Amore Mio*, please." She whispers on a shaky breath. His reluctance to move has Vanna stepping closer until she's standing in front of him with her hands cupping his cheeks. When she sees his face, a pained sob escapes her chest, and she collapses against him. Milo's hands dart out and catch her before she hits the floor. The pain in his expression when I get a glimpse of his face nearly breaks me.

My eyes dart to Michael as I feel Brittany and Jade's hands on me as they guide me to the couch. I feel Jade's shoulders shake while I stare emotionless at Michael who folds himself in half to sit on the coffee table in front of me.

"He called us an hour before we got there. We heard a crash and gunshots." The admission makes my stomach lurch in my gut. "We went to the scene and found Danny's body; Johnny is missing."

Chapter 36

Michael

My vision is a blurred haze of red, anger vibrates through me while I help Brittany and Mrs. D. get Nina into her and Johnny's room. I scoff internally at the thought, *Johnny* – when will the kid realize he hasn't been Johnny since he returned home. Nina is so tiny in my arms that she really does resemble Tinkerbell, or Tink, as Brittany calls her. As soon as they have the door open, I cross the room in a few long strides and gently place Nina on the bed. Her cat, Pinhead, hisses at me until he realizes I'm not a threat. His loud purr echoes through the room as he curls up next to his human. My eyes land on Mrs. D, the woman who helped raise Johnny. They say it takes a village, and in this life that couldn't be more true. I was young when the kid was born, but I took him under my wing the best I could. Knowing that he's out there on his own with a man who held his own blood captive and used her as a punching bag for years only serves to piss me off more.

I spin on my heel without a word toward the same way we came. My feet move with purpose as my mind reels with the list of things we have to do to fix this chaos. I hear Brittany's voice behind me talking to Mrs. D, but I don't register what she says until it's too late. The compact stick of dynamite that I haven't been able to stop thinking about since she first called me *Daddy* bounds across the room and stands in front of me. The door latch clicks in place when it's pulled closed, leaving us alone in the hallway.

"Michael, why am I here?" It's the first time I've ever heard the tiger refer to me by name. My God the sound of my name on her lips, my cock is weeping. Christ.

I lower my gaze to her, narrowing my eyes. When I saw her at the book shop with Nina, two things went through my mind. First, I can't leave Nina without a support system and second, I can't leave without knowing Brittany is safe. That is where I fucked up, because now, I won't let the woman out of this house until I know everything is settled and she'll be alright on her own. I don't give a shit who her mother is, she's too important not to look after myself. She has been taunting me every fucking time I've seen her. It's a shock I've lasted as long as I have without pulling some stupid shit like this.

"You know exactly why." I growl as I press her roughly against the wall and lower my lips to hers. My mouth captures hers in a possessive manner as I kiss the shit out of her. She melts into me, her fingers tangle in my short mane and she tugs as she tries to take control, which would normally lead to me turning a woman around and fucking her from behind against a wall, but I don't have that kind of time, and I need time to explore Brittany's body. A quickie in the middle of a hall when we're both stressed over Johnny's disappearance isn't the fucking time. I groan and pull away before I retreat to the office.

Milo is pacing the length of the room when I enter, his anxiety is rolling off him in waves. Ignoring him, I take a seat behind the desk and boot up the computer. I pull up several of the programs a tech wiz we've used in the past for hits we couldn't be associated with provided for us. Once it's up, I type in the information to load all security camera feeds at and near the parking garage where we found Danny's body. Now, it's a waiting game.

"I swear to God, you fucking pain in my ass, if you don't take a god damn Xanax and sit the fuck down, I'm going to kill you before Johnny gets a chance to do so for fucking Vanna." I snarl at Milo who is still wearing a dent into the hardwood floors.

The heat of his angry glare on the side of my face pulls my eyes away from the computer.

"She'll never forgive you if you are too worried about her to get him back. Get your shit together and let's do this." I stare at the kid I've trained to replace me when the time comes. He's nowhere near ready when this is his initial reaction.

Tens of thousands of images load from the area. Given it's city fucking hall, I'm not shocked. It takes Milo and I hours to review everything that has come up. I'm confused with what I see in some of the images, but the final location is exactly what I'd expect.

We've been waiting for nearly fifteen hours for visual confirmation. The cell phone ringing in my pocket pulls me from my task at hand. The task being pulling my hair out with fucking worry. I drag the device out and place it on the desk before swiping to answer. Once the call is placed on speaker, I speak.

"What?" I growl to the person on the other end.

"Confirmed with visual and thermal imaging. He's in Barone's basement." Abel's calm voice sounds from the other end of the phone.

Chapter 37

Nina

Flashes of memories continue to flicker through my mind. Beating after beating, any time I upset or inconvenienced the man that kept me isolated in the smallest of ways. They wouldn't even feed me properly, just enough to keep me alive. The knowledge I have now after my time training with Giovanni and Michael, I know that they made me work out so that I'd be too weak to try to fight back.

I feel the scream barreling up my throat only to get stuck. Nothing will come out; I'm lost so deeply in my own thoughts that my surroundings are a blur. Tears have been streaming down my cheeks since Michael told me he's missing, and I haven't been able to speak.

Anger radiates through my tiny frame when I realize that I've shrunk back into myself just like I had back then, when I was with them. The bed dips and I feel the presence of someone else near me, but I can't focus. My emotions are in a frenzy as I feel a soft cold hand cover my own. The cool skin against mine is enough to pull me from my thoughts, the darkness that I have been engulfed in begins to fade and I register Vanna.

Large red rimmed chocolate eyes that resemble his, stare at me through her own tears. She squeezes my hand tight as she places her other palm against my cheek, her concern for me as clear as her concern for her son. My shoulders begin to tremble as I let out a broken sob, one that has been building for too long.

"Sweetheart," the nurturing voice I know and love so much calls for my attention. "He needs you, I need you." She continues as she clasps both hands around mine. The anguish in her voice has my heart clenching. She continues with a hysterical sob, "He's been through more than one person should. He probably hasn't even told you because he's buried it for so long."

My eyes don't leave Vanna as she takes deep steadying breaths before continuing. I've never seen this woman look so broken or vulnerable. It's unnerving, and I hate everything about it.

"He doesn't know that I know Frederico forced him to kill my late husband. I planned to run, but the moment I put that plan into action Frederico was there." Vanna scoffs as she relives the memory. "He knew somehow and told me he would kill me if I tried to take his grandson. If I'd 'act up' he would threaten to hurt my Giovanni. Michael is the only one who could keep him from hurting either of us." Her confession breaks a piece of me while emboldening another. "Nina, you are the only one who can bring him back. Bring my Giovanni home, please."

It's as if Willow Rosenburg had just finished the spell to bring forth all of the potential Slayers when Brittany made me watch Buffy. I feel a sudden confidence and strength I didn't think I would ever possess. My arms fold around Vanna briefly before I release her and rush to where the men are holed up.

Hushed voices sound on the other side of the door when I approach Giovanni's office. I shove the door open not giving a single fuck about what they're talking about. When no less than six guns are pulled on me, I should be shocked or even scared. A normal person would be, right? Instead, I shrug my shoulders and stand in front of the desk with my spine straight. The men holster their weapons and go back to what they were doing when they realize I'm not a threat. At least not to them.

"What do you know?"

Michael glances back up from a blueprint with a cocked brow. "What do you mean?"

I feel the blood in my veins boil at his ridiculous question.

"You know damn well what I mean, Michael. Who has him and when do we leave to get him?" I snarl out my response.

Milo shoots up to his full height with a panicked look on his face. He glances between the men and me before he speaks.

"Uhhhh - Nina, you're not going anywhere. He'll kill us if you get hurt!" he stammers out his objection.

An unfamiliar maniacal laughter bubbles up from my chest.

"And you don't think I'll kill you if you don't let me in there?" My gaze must show the fire inside me when I speak. "Talk to Michael, he's been training me. If we had time, I'd prove it to you and lay your ass out right here." I motion to the floor in front of the desk. "But we don't and I'm not going to let anything more than what's already happened to him be done. So, I ask again. What. Do. You. Know?" I speak the question slowly, every word enunciated well enough that they understand just how serious I am.

The woman who stands before me is a stranger. I blink rapidly as I take in the reflection of the girl I used to be. I'm dressed in the sweatshirt and pants I haven't worn since the day I arrived here. Pride fills me at the realization that I'm not swimming in the material as I had before as I'm finally at a healthy weight. I take a deep breath before I leave the safety of our room to meet the men. The decision to leave while the rest of the house is still asleep was Michael's. He knows no one would let me out of the house if they had an inkling of what I was going to do.

Our drive to my childhood home feels like it takes twice as long as the first trip to the Ludovico's home was. My heart sinks as I recall that drive, Danny was the one behind the wheel. The memory only serves to add fuel to the anger that is already coursing through my veins.

Michael wastes no time when we pull up outside of the place I used to call home and makes the call. I see the front door swing open to reveal my father with a smug look plastered across his face. My entourage of misfits help me out of the car and create a protective shield around me as they escort me to where the man of my nightmares is looming. I can't help but recoil the closer we get to where he stands.

I force myself to relive every single time he hurt me as he leads us through the home. My third birthday was the first time I remember him hitting me. The day I had learned to read and was excited that he was there that day, how dare his own daughter show off her newly discovered skill. I was studying at my desk for a test Cece had planned for me the following day and even though I was in the middle of a sentence and didn't stand up the moment he walked into my room it was disrespectful. I was in so much pain I couldn't get out of bed for two days after that time. With Abel at my back, Rand and Milo part enough to allow me through to approach.

"Daddy," I say as sweetly and timidly as I can. His hand darts out and grabs me hard by the elbow. A pained hiss escapes which sends Abel into a frenzy.

"Don't fucking hurt her!" He screams at my father which only seems to make him tighten his hold on me.

Rand restrains Abel and says something quietly in his ear to make him calm, but his expression and demeanor are anything but friendly. I offer a reassuring smile to the brotherly figure, knowing that he's internally throwing every expletive at me for putting him in this position.

My father drags me through the house allowing the men to follow us. When we approach the room I had called home for so long, I freeze. A strong odor is coming from the place as he opens the door to reveal Cece. A loud scream barrels its way up my throat when I see the woman who raised me. My stomach lurches as I fight not to vomit. I see more bone than skin, what little skin is left makes her resemble *Imhotep* - before the full reincarnation. The only thing that clues me in to the identity is her hair. A throat clears somewhere behind me while my body is trembling with anger as I'm being held in place by a psychopath that I share half of my DNA with.

"We're not going to allow her out of our sight until we have our boss." Michael's tone is venomous as he speaks.

I feel my father lift his shoulders in a shrug as he drags me along behind him toward another door. He leads us down a narrow flight of stairs into a dimly lit, damp room. Before my eyes have a chance to adjust to the darkness, a light is turned on illuminating the room to show Giovanni chained to a metal chair. His beautiful brown eyes are hidden under swollen blue bruises. It's been two days since I've seen him and my body aches to be near him. The suit jacket and button up shirt he had on before he left is gone. His ink covered chest is hidden under layers of blood.

My eyes land on Michael who is standing stock still staring at his boss. I jerk my head for him to get Giovanni out. As soon as the men begin to move, I jerk my head back resulting in a forceful impact against my unsuspecting fathers face. His hold on my arm loosens enough for me to spin around and start whaling on him as I let out a scream that has been pent up for years. Every practiced punch, kick, and move that Michael had taught me, coming in clutch as I beat the man onto the ground. I'm not sure how much time has passed since he stopped trying to fight back when strong arms pull me off his limp body. Abel drags me out of the room, and I let out a defeated sigh.

"We've got Johnny. Let me get you." The urgency in his tone pulls me out of my spiral. "We'll come back and finish this later."

A subtle hint of lavender filters into my unconscious state. My cock pulses when the memories of Nina flood my thoughts. My desire quickly turns into anger when I realize it's not reality. Fuck, I miss her. It's been far too long.

I hear myself groan as the state of my body comes crashing down onto me as I come to. Every limb, organ, and nerve ending feels like it's on fire. The blankets that lay on top of me are too much, even the pressure of a sheet is too much. My body goes rigid when I realize I'm in a bed. My eyes fly open, and I begin to thrash around as a jolt of adrenaline courses through me. The attempt to get out of here is halted when a soft hand squeezes mine. That touch is the only thing that brings me down from the natural high.

"No, don't move. I'm right here." The sound of her voice is the sweetest thing I'll ever hear.

I turn my head to find Nina sitting next to me. She's dressed in one of my T-shirts, her elbows are leaning against the mattress with her fingers tangled around mine. My eyes rake up and down the little bit of her I can see, something has changed.

"*Amore Mio*," my voice is rough from lack of use. "What happened? How am I here? Where are the men?" I ask the questions without taking a breath or allowing her time to answer.

Her face falls as soon as the question passes my lips. The beautiful silver of her eyes has turned into a dark grey with the anxiety she's faced.

"Well, Michael and Rand are still trying to figure out what happened to my dad because his body was gone and with how badly I beat him, no one expected him to survive." Her cheeks flush as she makes the confession. "We didn't want to leave Vanna, Jade, and Brittany here alone to look further into it until we know where my father is."

My eyes widen when I realize what she just admitted. Before I pry for more information she continues.

"You were gone for two days. It was my fault." Her confession makes my heart stop. How the fuck could it be her fault. "I couldn't function; between their worry for me and the number of items they had to comb through, I was a distraction." Her shoulders begin to shake, she buries her face in our entwined hands as she sobs. "I'm so sorry, it was my fault you were hurt for so long."

A rumble of laughter climbs up my chest causing me to wince as it escapes. I shake my head in disbelief.

"*Bella*, had they not made sure you were ok before coming for me, I would be putting a bullet in every single one of my men right the fuck now." My lips turn up into a smile. I groan at the pain a simple fucking smile causes.

She grips my hand tightly as she stands and raises the other to cup my cheek. Tears spring to her eyes as she takes in my broken state. My eyes roam down her body and I notice discoloration on her elbow from this angle. As soon as I lift my hand and push the shirt up her arm, I see an angry bruise. My eyes light up with a fire as I take in the new information.

"Michael!" I roar the name like a goddamn lion. Nina flinches when my finger brushes against the tender skin.

"Nope. They've all been instructed not to enter this room unless I call for them." She announces with a confidence that is so fucking sexy.

"You were there, and he put his fucking hands on you. Why were you there?" I growl at Nina who is sitting patiently like she's speaking to a child.

"You saved me, Giovanni. You sent them to rescue me from that hell. A hell that you now have a glimpse of." She explains as her nostrils flare. "I know he doesn't play fair."

When I don't reply she rolls her eyes, clearly annoyed with me, and lifts the hem of my shirt exposing my stomach. It's covered in bruises, but also now has twelve identical twin marks scattered across my skin.

"Stun gun. The first time he used it on me he had beaten me so badly I already couldn't get out of bed for two days. That third day he used the stun gun on me expecting it to get me up and on the move. Spoiler - It didn't." Her chest sags as she lets out a deep breath. "Not long ago, you claimed me. You said you'd leave a trail of bodies if someone did something to me." She reminds me of the conversation we had just before her father interrupted us at dinner.

She leans in and presses a soft kiss against my swollen lips. I grip her neck and hold her in place as I savor every second. When she pulls away her eyes lock on to mine.

"I will kill my father for you, *Amore Mio*." Those silver eyes sparkle with so much unwavering adoration and loyalty as she speaks. Her sweet smile tugs at my heart. "We are in this together."

Nina has barely left my side, only long enough to shower. Hell, if the doctor that Michael brought in didn't personally tell her I was allowed to use a chair and sit in the shower to get cleaned up, she would have insisted on a sponge bath. She's walked in on me more than once stroking my dick too. It's been too long since I've had her, and fuck am I hard up, but she won't fuck me until I'm cleared. To say I'm in shock when my woman steps inside the shower with me is an understatement.

"What are you doing?" My voice is low and laced with need as my cock begins to stiffen.

She smiles sweetly at me while she kneels between my legs as the water streams down over her tight body. Her delicate hands grip my thighs as her eyes lock onto mine. The moment her nails dig into my flesh my dick pulses with anticipation.

"We may not be able to test my flexibility until you're given a green light, but that doesn't mean you need to suffer while we wait." She teases as she bends down and swipes her tongue across the throbbing head. "Just tell me what you like, Ok?" Her innocence and vulnerability make me feel like a jackass but the moment she pops the tip of my dick inside her mouth, I forget everything else.

A long groan rumbles deep within my chest as I fight every instinct to thrust up into her hot wet mouth.

"Fuck, *Amore*. Your mouth feels so good." I groan. "Flatten your tongue and take me a little deeper." I beg through a shallow breath.

She does as she's told, her tongue glides along the underside of my dick as she takes me deeper. The woman doesn't stop after a few inches though, no. She takes me as deep into her throat as she can, making a point to swallow around the head taking me a bit deeper. Son of a bitch. I'm going to last all of thirty seconds. My hands thread through her wet hair as I pull her back, but she refuses to let me take control and fuck, I think I fall even harder. Her nails dig harder into my thighs as she begins to bob her head.

"Nina," I pant her name as I feel that tingling sensation at the base of my spine. My balls begin to tighten. "*Bella*, I'm gonna –" My words are cut short when she takes me all the way back to her throat. Unable to hold myself back, my hands cup her head and hold her in place while I thrust into her throat. She hums around my cock and my vision goes fuzzy as my cock swells and pulses as I find my release.

When she finally sits back up, a wicked and proud smile splits her face as she wipes the tears that are streaming down her cheeks.

"Jesus Christ, woman, how the fuck was that your first time?" I pant as I help her stand and lower herself onto my lap. I bring her mouth to mine, my tongue swipes against her lips and she lets out a soft gasp as she allows me access. The taste of myself on her tongue makes me feral for her. She pushes me away after a moment when she realizes what I'm doing. The smile never falters as she cups my cheek.

"I may have been practicing." Her cheeks flush while I cock a brow at her in question. "When you've been napping, Brittany has been giving me pointers with one of the toys we bought."

Her admission has my dick immediately standing at attention again.

"You're going to be the death of me."

Chapter 39

Nina

It's been a week since Giovanni has been home. The doctor claims that he's cleared to get back to work and live life as he normally would. Part of me doesn't trust the man with a medical degree. I'm being overprotective but I hated seeing him in such pain. Today is the first day I've left his side, and that's only because I was conned by Michael. His praise over how I would be a great trainer for Brittany made me feel warm and fuzzy enough to agree to anything.

Since Brittany and I are roughly the same height, when she asked to borrow a pair of yoga pants and a sports bra for today I didn't think twice about it. But the moment I see her in the outfit she chose, I realize I'm going to have to lock the door to the gym while I show her the ropes. That is, at least, until she's allowed to get something to wear from home.

Her breasts are overflowing the small sports bra, and her round ass leaves nothing to the imagination in my pants. I'm most definitely jealous of how curvy she is. If any of the guys see her, Michael is going to unleash terror on the house. He really makes no sense to me. I hop out of the ring and move quickly to the door to lock it. She arches a brow at me in an unspoken question. The only way I can think to explain is to gesture to her tits as if she's Jessica Stanley at the Forks High School prom.

"You won't be the one paying the consequences if anyone else sees you in that." She and I both laugh as I climb back in.

I was asked in no uncertain terms by Michael to train Britt because he *"Will not allow either of you to be helpless should we be put in a dicey situation.*" The fact that he refuses to speak to her even though she flirts with him shamelessly confuses the hell out of me. According to Brittany, he's being a pussy. I don't really get the dynamic of their situationship as one may call it.

Brittany bounces back and forth on the balls of her feet trying to find the courage to swing at the mats I have on my hands. No matter how many times I've reassured her that it won't hurt me, she is fighting the process. My eyes nearly roll into the back of my head when she winds back only to relax her shoulders again before any impact can happen. I let out an annoyed groan.

"You think Michael's a pussy? You know you could have snuck into his room during the time you've been here." I taunt, trying to get her frustrated with me to want to hit me. "I guess you're all talk, huh – Mommy." I wiggle my brows at her, and she stops moving entirely with her mouth agape.

My friend doubles over in laughter at my words. When she stands up her eyes narrow into slits as she glares at me before she speaks.

"Whatever happened to the innocent and quiet girl? I miss her." She pulls her arm back and lands a right hook into my arm.

Ouch.

I stick my tongue at her like a teenager, which only ends up sending us both into a fit of laughter. As soon as we gather ourselves and get in a ready stance, my cell phone rings. I groan and pull off one of the pads before I rush over to the device. When I don't recognize the number, I tap the red button to ignore whoever is trying to get in touch with me. *They can leave a message.*

The only people I care to talk to on the phone are saved in my contact list. As I work to get the pad back on my hand my phone notification goes off again, the loud chime echoes through the room. This time it's for a text message; I glance down to the same number I don't have saved.

When I read the message, it takes me several tries to confirm I'm reading this correctly. My gaze darts up to find Brittany watching me curiously before I drag my eyes back to the screen.

Unknown:

> I have daddy dearest. If you want to end this with a bullet between his eyes and not your new little family – you're going to want to meet me here. We have some things to discuss.

Another message with a familiar address has me gasping for breath.

Johnny

A melodic tune fills the room as the hold music plays from my speakerphone. Peter has had me waiting for the past twenty minutes to speak with Mayor Ricci. The promise to provide her with more information in a timely manner is only serving to be a severe pain in my ass right now.

Milo and Abel are reviewing recent surveillance images, the two of them bent over the small table set in front of the couch. Rand is explaining the plan to the others who have been brought in on this, the same men who brought Nina to me. They're the only men I can trust to join us on this mission. Michael looms over the desk in front of me as I continue to wait.

"Hello Mr. Ludovico. It's nice to hear from you." The mayor's commanding voice chimes on the other end of the line while my office door crashes open simultaneously. The sound from the impact echoes around the room as Brittany stands drenched in sweat, her chest heaves as she takes in the group of ten men with guns aimed at her. Michael holsters his gun and pulls her into a protective hold while everyone else registers who just barged into my secure space. Once the threat has dissipated my friend releases the woman that he's not ready to admit is he wants.

"What is it, Britt?" I hear Michael's quiet question as I watch the exchange from where I stand waiting for my world to be destroyed.

"She's. Gone." Brittany pants out each word as she tries to catch her breath.

My body goes rigid, when my eyes find Michael, he's already turning toward the door to find her. Before he can step through the threshold, Brittany wraps her tiny hand around his large bicep which stops him in his track. I narrow my eyes on Nina's friend as I speak to the mayor who has been listening to the commotion.

"I apologize, Mayor Ricci, something urgent has come up. I will have to call you back." I press the button and end the call immediately after I finish my statement. I stand to my full height and cross my arms against my chest while I glare at Brittany. "You're going to want to talk really fucking fast since you won't let him leave to figure out where the fuck Nina went." I snarl.

"She's gone!" Brittany cries out as she continues, her hands moving wildly as she speaks. "She got a call from a number she didn't have saved, so she ignored it. Not five minutes later she received a cryptic text and bolted." The explanation doesn't do anything to comfort me. Brittany must realize I'm not happy with what she's shared because she holds up her hands in surrender with Nina's phone in her hand. I blink rapidly before I grab the device from her hand.

"What the fuck!" I snarl as I tap the screen furiously until I find her messages. I read the text and hand the device over to Michael. Anger pulses in my veins and I grab the closest thing to me, which happens to be a statue my grandfather had purchased years ago. I throw the heavy metal against the wall, the impact from my fury leaves a hole twice the size of the figure itself.

Brittany gasps and steps in the opposite direction just before she clears her throat to grab my attention again before she continues, "She took my phone. I assume so you had a way to track her. She shoved that into my hands after she snagged mine and bolted."

A deep growl reverberates through my chest as I begin to pace the length of the office. I feel everyone's eyes on me as my feet carry me back and forth across the room.

"What the fuck is she thinking?" A fire is lit in my eyes which only burns brighter when I hear a laugh from behind me. I spin on my heels to see an expression that matches my own emotions.

Michael chuckles darkly as he tests the weight of the phone in his hand. When he lifts his gaze to meet mine, he shakes his head.

"She's thinking that she wants revenge. Possibly more than you did when you returned." His insight startles me, and I freeze in my tracks. "He did some fucked up shit to her while she was growing up, hell even as recently as a week before we got her based on what she shared while we were training."

The darkness in his eyes has my skin prickling with tension. My imagination is getting the best of me knowing she's likely going into a fucking trap.

"He killed Cece and tried to shove Nina back into her old room where he left the body that is all but decomposed."

A guttural growl crawls up my throat as I take the phone back from Michael. When I read the address again something clicks, and I drop the device before I rush out of the room. I hear a stampede of footsteps rushing after me as I race toward my car.

As soon as I get behind the wheel of the black sports car I arrived here in what feels like a lifetime ago, I feel a sense of control. The moment the engine roars to life I slam my foot against the gas pedal and leave a cloud of dust in my wake. Knowing I have the mayor on my side that I can call in a favor if needed, I ignore every traffic law known to man as I drive across town. My fury only grows as I get closer to my destination as my imagination takes over with every fucked-up scenario that I could walk in to. When I finally pull up to the front door, I barely shift into park before I jump out of the car. The keys are still in the ignition as I pull the gun from the back of my waist band and prepare myself for what I am about to walk into as I open the door to Threads.

Chapter 41

Nina

My throat bobs as I swallow hard, steeling myself when I pull the door to Threads open. I knew I recognized the address. I've been here a total of two times since the incident. But each time, the familiar space with the beautiful aesthetic that Tabatha has created has welcomed me inside. The first time my experience was shrouded in a cloud of evil. My breath hitches as I step into the space and find that same evil standing next to my dad with his arm wrapped tightly around her waist. He looks better than he should, given how badly I beat him the last time we saw his face.

I take a step toward the woman who tried her damnedest to break me all those months ago. Her appearance hasn't changed much, apart from the way her hair is styled, now the platinum blond hair cascades in waves over her shoulders. However, there is a change she's not aware of which I'm reveling in. She doesn't realize I'm no longer the broken girl who was afraid of her own shadow. Now I'm a woman who will not hesitate to end someone who tries to hurt the people she loves.

"Janelle?" Her name holds a thousand questions.

The woman stares at me with a vile grin.

"You don't recognize Mommy, dear?" Her voice is laced with a fake sweetness that leaves my skin crawling.

My jaw drops to the ground, burrowing itself all the way to China. That's how shocked this revelation has made me.

"Sorry, what? I thought he killed you?" I shake my head and glance around her to find my father smirking like he's won the lottery.

Janelle meanders closer to me and slowly circles me like a predator who is ready to pounce on its prey.

"You see, I was never interested in being a mother." She admits as she looks me up and down. Her critical gaze looking for anything to taunt me with. "Daddy dearest over here begged me to go through with the pregnancy and said he'd take care of you. However, when he found out that you were going to be a girl, he couldn't bear to announce your existence to the world. Shame and all that misogynistic bullshit that comes with his lifestyle." Her explanation leaves me speechless.

My eyes gleam with unshed tears as I absorb everything this woman is sharing. I never thought that someone could be as evil as Mateo Barone. Fuck me, was I wrong.

"I asked him to spread the story that we both died during childbirth. He can bury you and I'd disappear. It wasn't until I returned with my partner to address some concerns about our business arrangement with Mateo that I found out you were still alive. He asked for my help when the Ludovico shithead took possession of you which is why I opted to get a job here with '*Auntie Tabs*,'" Janelle mocks the relationship Giovanni has with Tabatha, the owner of Threads, with air quotes. "You'd expect that their closeness would have been held under wraps, but no. It was easy to find after some cyber sleuthing. His mother was here almost daily for a visit until you arrived at their home."

She continues her trail around my still frame as she proceeds with the monologue she so clearly has been dying to have since she last saw me.

"My idea to abduct the Ludovico kid for my own vengeance, given how rudely he treated me the last time I saw you, was supposed to end with a trade for you. Not with this." She scoffs as she gestures to my dad who is still leaning against the counter. "I never expected when I ran out to grab lunch that I'd return to the mess you left." She stops moving and stands still with her eyes trained on me, a wide grin spread across her face. "That's when I decided I needed to make my existence known."

I let out a shaky breath as I absorb so much new information.

"Had that shithead's grandfather," she snarls as she points over my shoulder. I quickly glance to see Giovanni cautiously walking forward with a gun pointed at Janelle. "Had his grandfather not had the gambling problem he did, I never would have had to step a foot back in this god forsaken town." She snarls.

Giovanni stands close enough that I can see the confused expression on his face now. Janelle snorts before she continues, her attention entirely on him now.

"Your grandfather made so many bets with my partner over the past few years he was about to lose everything before we brought the opportunity to Mateo." Her confession seems to spark something in him which she hasn't realized because she continues to run her damn mouth. "I knew he would be a good lap dog and do as he was told. Helping us get the drugs into the city so that we could both make money. It was my way of apologizing for making him kill his daughter, only color me surprised when I find out that she's alive and well enough to be used as a bargaining chip. Or alive at least. Though, you do look a little better than the last time I was forced to look at you."

I roll my neck to loosen the tight muscles her yammering has caused. When she turns back to me, I offer my most innocent smile which seems to infuriate her enough to approach me. Before she has a chance to continue her speech, I do what I should have done before she began talking. I pull the gun I grabbed from the armory in the gym and lift it in front of me.

Janelle's eyes go wide just as I squeeze the trigger. A loud shot sounds and reverberates through the space. Thankfully the secret practices I've been having with Michael have paid off because my aim is true and hits right between the eyes.

"You talk too much." I groan and roll my eyes as she falls to the ground.

Present Day

I drag my blood-stained fingers through my hair as I think about everything that's happened since I killed the head of the Ludovico family while I stare at Mateo Barone who is tied to the same metal chair he had me confined to not so long ago. Ahh, karma. She's such a team player.

"It seems only fair that you be one of the first to know, after all. You're the one who killed him, so to speak." My lips turn up as I aim a devilish smile his way, recalling everything that has happened. The fact that his daughter is now mine in nearly every way only makes this moment better. "Johnny is gone."

I see the recognition as a glint of fear appears in his eyes. My desire to taunt him even further gets the best of me as I bend to speak directly into his ear. "This is the moment where if I respected you, I'd ask your permission." I grin darkly. "However, you're the worst kind of trash that I've come across so I'm just going to tell you. One day soon, I'm going to propose to your daughter. She will become a Ludovico, and your name will be forgotten." A low grumble erupts from deep in his chest which brings me so much joy.

My feet carry me over to the door that closes off the room to the onlookers. While we may plan to burn this place to the ground, I don't want to leave any chance that this fucker gets away. Plus, I came here for vengeance after all.

The moment I place my hand on the doorknob, I feel a sense of pride run through me. He has no idea what he's in for. If I'm honest, neither do

I. The door pulls toward me easily and Nina steps into view. The same set of clothing she wore when she first came to me.

She has an air of confidence about her now though that no one can take. Between all of the work she's already done, there's also just something about your first kill that does that to you. Nina's feet move swiftly as she closes the distance between herself and the bloody sack of bones in the middle of the room.

I lean back against the wall with my arms folded across my chest, savoring my chance to observe her. Barone's eyes go wide when he realizes what she has.

"Hi, Daddy," Nina's voice is sweet and timid, she's putting on a show for him. "Do you remember the first time you used this one on me?" She reveals the same taser Mateo used on me a little over a week ago from the pocket of her sweatpants. I stifle a laugh while my eyes roam from her to him. The man looks like he's ready to blow a gasket.

"I was three years old; it was just after I finished my cake." She seems almost ashamed as she speaks. "Cece had made it for me, she said it was our secret because you didn't approve of cake."

A loud crackle echoes through the empty space when she presses the button to activate the device. The action illuminates Mateo's grim expression, he looks almost remorseful when he realizes the power that she now has over him. She steps into his space and presses the prongs to his thigh for the count of three before she releases the trigger. He lets out a shrill scream that continues to ring through the room after he's stopped.

"Three years old and you used a fucking taser on me because you didn't want my birth to be celebrated, for reasons I didn't know at the time. Now I realize it's because of what I'm lacking between my god damn legs." Nina scoffs, "You know, she told me once that you were her big brother and that's why she wouldn't leave me because she knew what you were capable of. Even if it meant she had to suffer at your hands too."

Nina shoves the prongs into his neck this time before pressing the button that brings it to life. This time the screams and noise from the taser don't stop for the count of six. She has a single tear streaming down her cheek when she pulls away.

"You know, something has been bothering me since I was last here. I don't understand why she didn't leave when I got away." Her admission comes out on a shaky breath. "How soon after they took me home did you kill her?"

Mateo glances up at her with tears and snot running down his face, not from guilt or remorse, but from the pain she's inflicted. If looks could kill, the furious glare he's shooting at her would have had Nina laid out flat. Every fiber of my being wants to end this now and use my knife to slit his throat all the way through to the bone. However, I made a promise, and I know she needs this closure so I will bide my time.

"The day you left," he chokes on a laugh. "There was no point to keep her alive anymore." He struggles to shrug his shoulders with the restraints.

Nina's eyes are ablaze with fury. Her gaze meets mine and she subtly jerks her head signaling me to join her. Her body sags into me with relief as soon as she feels me step behind her.

"I hope you and my mother both rot in hell." Are the last words she says to him before stepping aside. A wicked smile dances across my lips as I pull the Glock from the back of my waistband, aim, and shoot without any further hesitation.

Nina turns to me, her eyes rimmed with tears as she buries her face into my chest.

"*Amore Mio.*" I wrap her in my arms, holding her to my chest as she lets out the excess emotion this kill has caused her.

Epilogue

Nina

Nine Months Later

Part of me wishes I'd have worn something a bit warmer. The black off the shoulder sweater dress is sexy, especially the matching knit stockings, but it's already windy as hell on the sidewalk. My gaze drags up the building toward the roof. It's going to be an ice box up there.

Giovanni's fingers are tangled around mine as he drags me inside the hotel. Abel and Rand follow closely behind us as we approach the elevator. I lean into my man's warmth as we wait for the car to arrive. It's nearly our second Christmas together so the fact that he wanted to spend the night before Christmas Eve here, instead of wrapping gifts or just with our family, has my mind racing. Last year may have been a little more hectic considering my father was trying to kill us both and all that shit. But it was my first time celebrating with a family.

The doors open slowly, Giovanni gestures for me to go in ahead of him. Once he's standing at my side, Abel and Rand step in after creating a human shield in front of us. Rand presses the button for the rooftop bar. Shockingly, the ride to the top is quick and not as terrifying as I had expected.

Giovanni's hand presses gently on the small of my back as he guides me toward the door that takes us to the outside patio. I gasp as I take in the space that is dotted with enclosed igloos, just big enough for two. I turn to face him with a mixture of anticipation and displeasure. He looks just as confused as I feel.

"What is it, Short Stack?" His smooth voice sounds as he bends down to speak into my ear.

"You're not going to make them stand outside in this cold while we're in one of these are you?" I scold Giovanni which causes laughter to erupt from him and the two men who have sworn to protect us this evening.

"No, *Amore Mio*, they're staying inside. Apart from Jordon who will be our server, no one else will be permitted access to the rooftop this evening." He presses his lips to my jaw with a quick kiss before he leads me further onto the roof. We don't stop until we're at an enclosed dome that is situated in a way that we somehow still have a view of the river below.

My breath hitches as we walk into the structure. A lit Christmas tree and fairy lights complete the ambiance of the space. I take a seat on the couch where Giovanni meets me a moment later. I'm not used to the laid-back look he's sporting tonight, but I'm a fan; I thought he looked good in a suit, but his ass in those jeans. Fuck, it should be illegal to look so good in clothes *and* out of them. As if he's reading my thoughts, he shrugs off the dark sports coat he's wearing over a dark Henley, halfway unbuttoned. As soon as his arms are free, I audibly gulp. Over the past year he's somehow become even more muscular, and his ink covered, corded forearms have a way of making me melt.

"What is it?" He taunts me with a knowing wink.

My brain misfires and words fail me, I groan as he chuckles and pulls me into his arms. A moment later he drapes a warm fuzzy blanket over our laps as we bask in the silence and enjoy a moment to ourselves with no one else around for a long time. Just as I'm about to speak, a woman unzips the entrance to our little love bubble. She's stunning, with a flawless dark complexion. Long raven braids hang down her back while her large brown eyes sparkle with an infectious joy as she approaches us with a beautiful bottle in her hand.

"Hi y'all. My name is Jordon, I'll be taking care of you two this evening." She presents the bottle she was cradling to show a Crisp Apple Wine from a local winery. My eyes dart to Giovanni who has a sly smile pulling at his lips. "This is one of the most popular wines we have." She reassures, not realizing the last time this man tried to get me to drink I nearly spat it all over him.

"Thank you, Jordon." His chuckle warms my insides, "You can leave the bottle, I'll pour it."

She grins knowingly at us before retreating from the igloo. My cheeks flush when I realize where her mind went. I mean she's not wrong. It's not like this is even the most public place we've had sex in the last year.

The pop of a cork drags me from my thoughts. My lips turn up at the corners when Giovanni hands me a glass of wine. I quirk a brow at the beautiful man who leans in and presses a soft kiss to my lips before pulling away. His way of telling me to trust him. I roll my eyes and lift the glass to my lips before taking a long pull. He must notice my surprise by the chuckle that escapes him. Before he can stop me, I finish the contents of the glass.

"Oh boy, you're going to feel that in a minute." He snorts and pulls me back into him.

I'm not sure how much time has passed since time seems to have gone hazy when Jordon returns to drop off an order of naan bread. My stomach growls as I grab the bowl and take a large bite. I groan around the mouthful of buttery goodness.

"Why is this so good?" I ask as I chew.

His answering laugh brings me to a fit of giggles. I lean back into his warm chest and savor the feel of his steady heartbeat against my spine.

"What made you decide to come here?" I finally get out the question that's been on my mind all night. "I loved being with your mom and Jade this time last year." I admit sheepishly.

Giovanni's lips dance with amusement as he adjusts himself to face me. His large hands envelop mine while his eyes stare through the wall of insecurities I haven't been able to knock down completely.

"We will spend the next few days with them. I needed time for just us." His lips find mine and my eyelids flutter closed while we're connected for the briefest of moments before he slides away from me. My body begging for more of his attention elicits a groan from my needy mouth as soon as his warmth is gone.

When my eyes open again, I see the beautiful man who has rescued me in so many ways kneeling before me. His chocolate eyes sparkle as the beautiful mouth that was just on mine turns up into a sinful grin.

"Short Stack, I don't know how to say this without just saying it." His admission makes my stomach flop, the earlier wine ready to make a reappearance. "I had no plan to stay here after Frederico was taken care of. After Lucia – fuck. I never thought I'd be interested in anyone for more than a warm body again."

I squirm under his gaze. His warm smile does little to calm me until he leans in for another soft kiss.

"What I'm trying to say is, I never wanted to be Capo." He chuckles and lifts a hand from where it's laying on top of mine to drag through his unruly hair. "But in my ascension to the throne, I have found my queen."

My hands fly to my chest when he lifts a ring box that he's had hidden under the blanket. He pops the top open, revealing a simple platinum solitaire diamond ring. Tears sting the corners of my eyes as I nod my head to say yes as the words are lodged in my throat. His smile widens even more, one with so much pride that I haven't seen before. One that I can't wait to see every day for the rest of our lives.

"My king," the thought springs free from my lips. I giggle as silent tears of joy fall down my cheeks. He slides the beautiful ring onto my left hand before he stands and pulls me up into his arms. The rest of the evening is spent in each other's embrace while we finish the bottle of wine and dream of what the future holds.

My sole purpose in life, outside of the Ludovico family, is her. It's been her for the nearly two years that she's been in my life. The first time I laid eyes on her, she called me Daddy. The only thing I've been able to think of since is filling her with my seed and making her mine. If only that were an option.

My place in the shadows is comforting and familiar as I track her movements through the ballroom. Her hair is still as vibrant a pink as the first day we met, styled in soft waves down her back. My cock has been hard as stone, straining against the zipper of my pants after seeing the dress she chose for tonight. Brittany steps more clearly into my line of sight, giving me another look at the strappy black fitted evening gown she's wearing. The sweetheart neckline, which frames her perky tits to perfection, is the only conservative aspect of the damn thing. Thin straps of fabric crisscross all the way from her shoulders to her lower back which is where the plunging scoop ends, just above the swell of her ass. Every sliver of skin that is on display shows off her deliciously designed tattoos. Her body is a canvas and my favorite work of art.

A groan escapes as soon as I see his stupid ass face walk up beside her. My lips pull into a snarl when I see his hand graze her skin. That slimy weasel has been the bane of my god damn existence since her step-mother introduced them. I've spent more time than I care to admit looking into his background. It's like he vanished after high school; there's nothing more recent than the Port Windsor High transcripts. Which tells me jack shit that I didn't already know. After all, my boss had more than one run in with the shit head when they were kids. I've never been so grateful to have the less than savory contacts that I do after being a part of this lifestyle for so long. Being able to reach out to a young woman who is even better with computers than I am should give me the answers I'm looking for soon.

His mouth is entirely too close to her neck. My hand wraps so tightly around the steering wheel of my SUV that the leather creaks. Thankful I'm stuck in the shadows outside tonight because my control is obviously wavering where she's concerned. She's been seeing Peter for a few weeks now, constantly joining him for events that Mayor Ricci is attending. Even though Giovanni warned her about him, she still decided to play matchmaker with her step-daughter.

My vision blurs with rage when I see him go in for the *kill* so to speak. Nausea rolls through me as I witness their first kiss. She doesn't appear to respond as beautifully as she did with me. The thought takes me back to our first kiss which is also the last time I've touched a woman for more than the sparring sessions I have with Nina, my boss's fiancé.

A year and a half ago

"Michael, why am I here?" It's the first time I've ever heard the tiger refer to me by name. My God the sound of my name on her lips, my cock is weeping. Christ.

I lower my gaze to her, narrowing my eyes. When I saw her at the book shop with Nina, two things went through my mind. First, I can't leave Nina without a support system and second, I can't leave without knowing Brittany is safe. That is where I fucked up because now, I won't let the woman out of this house until I know everything is settled and she'll be alright on her own. I don't give a shit that she's the mayor's step-daughter, she's too important not to look after myself. She has been taunting me every fucking time I've seen her. It's a shock I've lasted as long as I have without pulling some stupid shit like this.

"You know exactly why." I growl as I press her roughly against the wall and lower my lips to hers. My mouth captures hers in a possessive manner as I kiss the shit out of her. She melts into me, her fingers tangle in my short mane and she tugs as she tries to take control which would normally lead to me turning a woman around and fucking her from behind against a wall but I don't have that kind of time and I need time to explore Brittany's body. A quickie in the middle of a hall when we're both stressed over Johnny's disappearance isn't the fucking time.

Present Day

I haven't been able to stop myself from thinking about that kiss at least three times a day since it happened. My cock hasn't stopped weeping for her since that exchange. The way her tight body melted into me so perfectly is what wet dreams are made of. Trust me, I'd know. I've woken up every goddamn morning with a sticky mess on my stomach having come in my sleep from the memories of her body pressed so firmly against mine alone.

If only she were meant to be mine.

She's nearly half my age and with my line of work, having someone I care about woven too tightly into my life would put her in far too much danger.

So, instead of giving into the temptation that is the beautiful goddess of a woman I can't get out of my mind, I watch from afar when she can't know that I'm here to ensure her safety.

To Nicole, who has begged me for Johnny's story since she first read The Unexpected Match.

My family, your support during this journey has been incredible.

To my Stupid Face Moron, ditto.

My alpha team, you are the MVP, and I can't imagine this journey without you.

Sara - My boo. I'll forever be thankful that you slid into my DM's. You are phenomenal, and I love you!

Brittany – From 0-2mil and for the rest of the ride. You are one of my favorite humans and I'm so thankful to know you…. & for Abelina.

Tana – I'll never be able to thank you enough for the way you've curbed the chaos that is my mind.

K.D. - My ride or die, I love you, and I'm so freaking proud of you!

My Street Team – Bestie Boo's:

Laura P., Jordon S., Brittany T., Jennifer L., Megan A., Brandy S., Nicole H., Ashley P., Lori L., Morgan H. Leigh U., Cheryl P., Jessi H., Tabs S., Haley E., Nicole W., Jasmine G., Jeanette R., Erin V., Becci T., Courtney C., Tiffiany S., Lindsey M., Nickol D., Veronica T., Sidhi B. Without y'all I don't know where I'd be. You are the best group of people a girl could ask for. <3

While the Under The Cover bookstore in this book is fiction, it is a nod to the wonderful romance book store in Kansas City, MO, who was the first store to take a chance on me and my books. I will be forever thankful to Carley for that.

To the FBI Agent who tracks my search history, it's been real.

Lastly, but most definitely not least, to every single one of you who has reached this page. There will never be enough words for me to express my love for you adequately. Thank you for reading my books. I can't wait to share additional stories with you!

I'm an introvert. Well, until you get to know me. Then I won't shut up. I'm married to my favorite PITA; he's the doctor to my Clara. (IYKYK). We have a little boy who is growing way too fast and is already way too smart for my own sanity. I've had an unhealthy obsession with *Gilmore Girls* and *Buffy the Vampire Slayer* for years. You'll see the references throughout my writing. I've loved reading for as long as I can remember, but physical books with traditional novel paper give me the ick! So, you'll find me reading on my Kindle or listening to audiobooks on the regular.

Be sure to stalk me on all of my socials here